THREE PICKLED HERRINGS

WINGS & CO.

THREE PICKLED HERRINGS

BOOK TWO

Sally Gardner

illustrated by David Roberts

SQUARE
FISH

Henry Holt and Company
New York

SQUARE FISH

An Imprint of Macmillan
175 Fifth Avenue
New York, NY 10010
mackids.com

Square Fish books may be purchased for business or promotional use.
For information on bulk purchases, please contact the Macmillan Corporate
and Premium Sales Department at (800) 221-7945 x5442 or by e-mail at
specialmarkets@macmillan.com.

Library of Congress Cataloging-in-Publication Data is available.

ISBN 978-1-250-06438-7

Originally published in the United States by Henry Holt and Company, LLC
First Square Fish Edition: 2015
Book designed by Ashley Halsey
Square Fish logo designed by Filomena Tuosto

10 9 8 7 6 5 4 3 2 1

LEXILE: 700L

For my darling friend, who I'd be lost without,

Rosa Weber

—S. G.

THREE PICKLED HERRINGS

WINGS & CO.

Chapter One

Mrs. Fosset was on the first-floor landing, duster in hand, when the clock in the hall started to chime.

"Nine o'clock," she said out loud to the curtains and the chair.

From the window she watched her employer, Sir Walter Cross. He was at the bottom of the garden by the frozen duck pond, feeding his ducks. As always, he was standing by the old weeping willow, which this morning had a layer of frost over its branches. Doughnut, his faithful miniature dachshund, was jumping up and down and barking, the funny little thing.

"You could time an egg by the old boy, and it would

never be hard-boiled," said Mrs. Fosset. "A man of regular habits."

There were some strange things about Sir Walter's regular habits. First of all, come rain or shine, he always took with him a toy umbrella. It was a mystery to Mrs. Fosset. It wouldn't keep the rain off a garden gnome. Then there was his strict rule that nobody else should be allowed in the garden while he fed his ducks. After fifteen months of working for the elderly bachelor, Mrs. Fosset still had no idea why.

It was as the last chime sounded from the hall clock that something extraordinary happened. Sir Walter Cross appeared to rise out of his walking boots, purple smoke curdling from his red-socked feet. He rose into the air, slowly at first, and then seemed to perform the impossible magic trick of hovering about a foot above the ground. Faithful Doughnut barked furiously and jumped up until he managed to attach his gnashers to the bottom of Sir Walter's trouser leg. Pulling with all his might, he tried to bring his owner back down to earth.

At first it looked as if the brave hound might succeed, but firecrackers burst from Sir Walter's feet

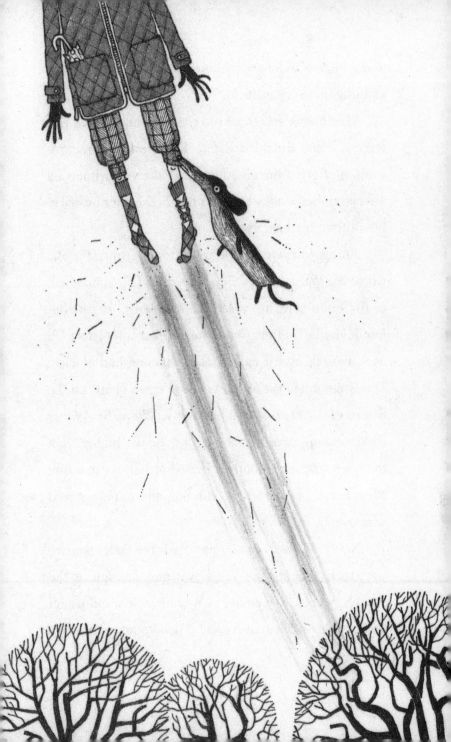

and both dog and master whooshed skyward, Doughnut clinging on for dear life.

Mrs. Fosset was frozen to the spot, helpless, as this terrible scene unfolded before her eyes. Not being a woman of great imagination, what she was witnessing seemed unbelievable. She clutched her feather duster to her bosom, her knees weak.

Things outside the window took a turn for the worse. Sir Walter's trouser leg ripped, and Doughnut fell, at first with startling speed, back down to earth. But just before he hit the ground, he stopped completely. To Mrs. Fosset's eye, it looked as if someone had plucked Doughnut out of the air and set him down gently on the frozen grass. He was still barking wildly as Sir Walter continued upward, higher than the house, higher than the trees. He was shouting, but what he was shouting Mrs. Fosset couldn't hear through the double-glazed window.

Never in her whole life had the housekeeper seen such a sight. Sir Walter was now as high as the church steeple, suspended in midair as if standing on an invisible platform in the sky. Then, to her horror, Sir

Walter lost his balance. Trailing rainbow colors behind him, he fell as a stone might. No stopping for him, no— he fell splat to the ground as a dazzling display of stars whizzed into the cold, gray morning sky.

In a terrible state, Mrs. Fosset called for an ambulance and the police while the young gardener, Derek Lowe, who was in the kitchen, ran to the bottom of the garden. He found Sir Walter at the edge of the duck pond, neatly laid out, his boots facing the water, his stockinged feet pointing skyward. He was dead. Doughnut had vanished.

Chapter Two

Detective James Cardwell arrived at Sir Walter Cross's Georgian mansion to find that Sergeant Litton of the Podgy Bottom Police had got there well before him. Detective Cardwell had a low opinion of the potato-faced sergeant.

"I have this under control," said Sergeant Litton, stamping his feet on the ground and rubbing his hands together as watery flakes of snow began to fall. "Blooming cold. The sooner we wrap this up the better."

"How did he die?" asked Detective Cardwell.

"It appears the gentleman just dropped down dead," replied Sergeant Litton.

"Did anyone see anything?" asked Detective Cardwell.

"There are no suspicious circumstances, I can assure you of that," said Sergeant Litton.

"What does his housekeeper—Mrs. Fosset—say?"

"Some rubbish about Sir Walter whizzing up into the air with his dog attached to his trouser leg. The woman is bonkers. You can't believe a word she says. I mean, no one can just whiz up into the air. It's not possible."

James Cardwell bent down and carefully examined the body.

"Where's the dog now?" he asked.

"Ran away," said the sergeant. "Look, there's no more to this than meets the eye." He laughed. "The only thing I'd like to know is which horse he'd backed for the two-thirty at Cheltenham."

"You like a flutter on the horses?" asked Detective Cardwell.

"No, I'm not a gambling man," said the sergeant, "but it wouldn't be betting, would it? I'd be backing a surefire winner. Sir Walter Cross was famous for his golden knack of picking a winner every time."

Detective Cardwell said nothing. He stood for a few minutes, looking out at the duck house, before slowly walking all the way around the pond. He felt his fairy wings begin to flutter under his shirt. After waiting a hundred years to have his wings returned to him, it was a sensation that he was becoming used to again. Whenever things weren't right, they began to quiver— and there was something decidedly wrong with this case. Fortunately, it was cold enough that he needed to wear a heavy overcoat. It would be a problem to explain flapping wings to the sergeant. Or, for that matter, to anyone in the police force. He was near a clump of bulrushes when he bumped into the gardener.

"Strange business," said Derek Lowe.

"Indeed," said Detective Cardwell. "Did you see what happened?"

"No, I didn't. Mrs. Fosset did, though, and she isn't a woman who goes about inventing nonsense. She said the old boy went up like a rocket and came down like a rock."

"So I've heard," said Detective Cardwell. "You were the first to see the body?"

"Yes—and I could see Sir Walter's footprints," said the gardener. "They were clearly outlined in the frost, and so were Doughnut's. Sir Walter wouldn't allow anyone into the garden while he fed his ducks. But I can't explain this: next to where he lay was a trail of small footprints that led to the willow tree and no farther. I mean, people don't just pop up and vanish again, do they?"

James Cardwell's wings were now definitely twitching.

"Thank you," he said. "You have been most helpful. Will you tell Mrs. Fosset I would like to see her?"

Fairy meddling, thought Detective Cardwell as he rejoined Sergeant Litton. *This case has all the hallmarks of fairy meddling.*

Chapter Three

The fairy detective agency, Wings & Co., had been open for business for five months, and so far they had not had one case.

Emily Vole, at the tender age of nine, had inherited the shop from her dear friend Miss String. Emily often thought that if it hadn't been for Miss String and Fidget, she might still be nothing more than a servant to her horrid ex-adoptive-parents-slash-employers, Daisy and Ronald Dashwood, and their triplets. Now everything had changed for the better. There was only one small gray cloud in her otherwise blue sky. Well, maybe two, if you took into account Buster Ignatius Spicer.

Emily sighed. She thought that Buster would be a

bit more concerned that so far they had not had one case.

"Aren't you worried by all this nothing business?" she asked.

Buster, who was eleven and had been eleven for the past one hundred years, said unkindly, "You are only worried because you are a human being and have a life span. We fairies don't."

"Oh dear. I know I'll be all grown up by the time we finally have a case," said Emily.

"I doubt that, my little ducks," replied Fidget the cat. "I think something is going to come along. Call it animal instinct."

"When?" asked Emily impatiently.

"When" turned out to be a snowy Wednesday. Fidget was polishing the curious cabinets in the shop when the bell rang. There, half in, half out of the doorway, under a black umbrella, appeared a round gentleman. His shoes were so well polished that Fidget could see the end of his tail in them.

The round gentleman slowly folded his umbrella.

"Come in," said Fidget, adding, "A good day for fish."

"Strike me pink," said the gentleman, looking Fidget up and down. "You're a fancy-dress outfitter, aren't you? I thought so when I first peered through the window."

"No," said Fidget. "We are a fairy detective agency. The only one in Podgy Bottom."

The gentleman thought about that carefully before introducing himself as one Mr. Rollo, a tailor.

"I used to do a lot of work for the theater. If they saw that costume of yours, well . . . ," he said. "You're not in the theatrical business then?"

Fidget assured him that they were neither theatrical costumers nor fancy-dress suppliers, then asked, "What can I do for you, Mr. Rollo?"

Mr. Rollo looked uncertain that a cat the height of

a man could do anything for him, even if he was a very well-dressed cat and had good manners.

"I don't rightly know. Well," he said, "maybe it's all hocus-pocus." Seeing the curious cabinets that lined the shop, he asked, "What's in those, if you don't mind my asking?"

"Fairy wings," said Fidget.

"Oh!" The tailor laughed. "That's a good one. And what do they do, these fairy wings?"

"They don't do anything. They can't," said Fidget, and explained to Mr. Rollo how each pair of wings was locked away in a drawer and each drawer had its own key.

"Only when a key takes it into its metal-brained head to unlock the drawer is the fairy who owns the wings called back to collect them," said Fidget. "But there's a problem. The keys are a contrary bunch of whitebait, and they don't do what they're told. Emily Vole, the Keeper of the Keys, asks them very kindly, but so far they have only brought back one detective and a solicitor, much to the frustration of all the other fairies."

"That cheers me up, that really does," said the tailor. "What a tall story."

Fidget showed Mr. Rollo to a chair.

"What's your story, then?" Fidget asked, as he made the tailor a cup of tea and a fish paste sandwich.

"Well, I suppose nothing can top fairy wings and metal-brained keys."

"Spot on the fishcake," said Fidget.

"Well," said Mr. Rollo, his face sad, "everything has gone bottoms up, so to speak."

And he began to tell Fidget his sorry tale.

He had a tailor's shop in the high street. Once, not long ago, everything was going so well. The order books were full, and there was even a waiting list.

With the money he made from his business, he and his wife had been able to buy their dream home. All their wishes had come true. Then suddenly, for no reason that Mr. Rollo could pinpoint, all his customers went elsewhere, even the ones on the waiting list. The theater stopped employing him. They said he had left pins

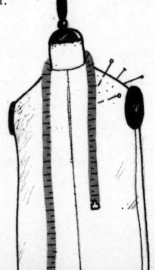

in the costumes. As if that wasn't bad enough, the dream house was discovered to have been built on marshland that no one knew was there. With no money coming in, Mr. Rollo had been forced by the bank to put the house up for sale. But who wanted to buy a sinking building?

"As for the shop," said Mr. Rollo, "it, too, will have to be sold. What more can I say but . . . well?"

Fidget thought everything sounded most unwell. In fact it smelled fishy, very fishy indeed.

"This is a very pickled herring if ever I saw one," he said.

"It is," said Mr. Rollo.

"Don't worry. You've come to the right place," said Fidget reassuringly.

"I have?" said the tailor, surprised.

"Yes. We will take the case."

"What case?" asked Mr. Rollo.

"Why," said Fidget, "the case of who stole your good luck."

"You can do that?" asked Mr. Rollo, a smile breaking out on his worried face. "You don't think it to be impossible?"

"No," said Fidget. "We are, after all, a fairy detective agency."

"Well, there's a thing," said Mr. Rollo. "And I only came in to admire your costume."

As he left, he nearly bumped into Detective Cardwell.

"Our first case, Jimmy," said Fidget, greeting the detective.

"Good," said James Cardwell. "And I have brought you another one. This one is decidedly fishy."

"Don't tell me," said Fidget. "It's a pickled herring."

Chapter Four

mily Vole was curled up on the sofa in the living room above the shop, reading a book on how to become a detective. She sighed, put it down, and looked at the keys. Proper detectives didn't have to deal with a bunch of keys that stubbornly refused to open drawers. Proper detectives had dead bodies to worry about and things like that, while Emily worried about all the fairies who were desperately waiting for their wings to be returned.

The keys sat in a row on the armchair next to her, their boots all neatly laced, and beside them was the magic lamp, its little feet in their Moroccan slippers

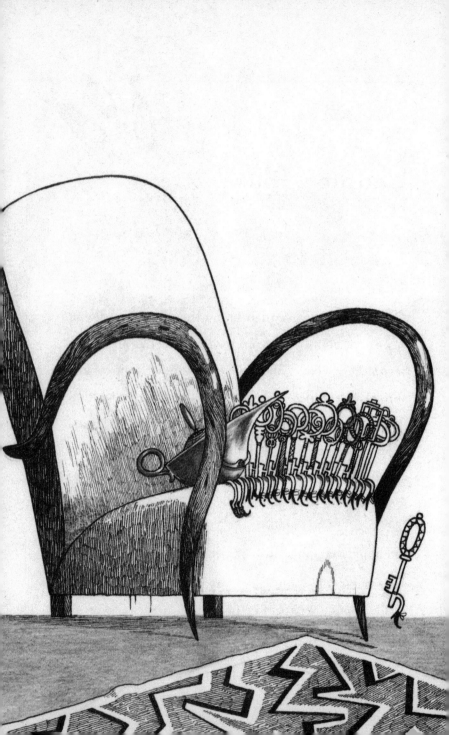

swinging to and fro, its little arms folded over its golden tummy.

She felt sorry for the magic lamp. It had a troubled past. Once it had been in the employment of the witch, Harpella, who had used it wickedly, but now it was Emily's most devoted fan.

"If you were a fairy detective," said Buster Ignatius Spicer, "you wouldn't need to go reading books and stuff. Like me, you would just know what to do."

"If you're so smart," said Emily, "then solve the mystery of why the keys won't open another drawer."

"That's your job, not mine," said Buster bitterly, for he resented the fact Emily had been left the detective agency in the first place. After all, she didn't even belong to the fairy world.

Buster was not in a good mood that day. But then good moods and Buster didn't often go together. He hated being eleven. He had been eleven for more than one hundred years, since Harpella cast a spell on him. He was doomed to stay that way for ever and ever. And if that wasn't bad enough in the great scheme of things, the keys simply refused to open the drawer and give his wings back to him.

"It's because you are a human," continued Buster, "and don't understand fairy ways and never will—"

"Birdcage," interrupted Emily. She said it again. "Birdcage."

"That's not fair," replied Buster.

Emily picked up her book once more. Chapter fourteen, "Clues."

"It was the only mistake I ever made," said Buster. "I bet you've made loads of mistakes."

"None as stupid as shrinking myself to the size of a doll and being imprisoned in a birdcage," said Emily over the top of her book.

"It was a goblin who shrank me," said Buster. "If I'd had my wings, it would never have happened."

"You were stuck until Fidget and I saved you. And the lamp undid the spell so that you became the right size again."

"He never even said thank you," piped up the magic lamp.

"Oh, put a genie in it," said Buster.

Emily giggled.

"It's no laughing matter," said Buster. "If you were a proper Keeper of the Keys, I would have my wings back by now."

"And if you were a proper detective, you would know why—"

"Ah, here's the living room." Detective Cardwell poked his head around the door.

"James, I'm so pleased it's you!" Emily jumped off the sofa and was caught by the detective, who swung her around the room.

"Hello, Buster. Still as grumpy as ever, I see," he said as he put Emily down.

"There's not much to be cheerful about, James," said Buster. "Unless you count trying to solve the matter of why the keys won't open another drawer, we haven't had a single case."

"Well, you do now. I have one for you," said Detective Cardwell.

Fidget came in carrying a tray of tea, buns, strawberry jam, sponge cake, and fish paste sandwiches.

"And I have another one," he said. "A tailor—"

"You mean someone actually came through the shop door asking for our help?" said Emily excitedly. Something at last was happening.

"Spot on the fishcake, my little ducks," replied Fidget.

They all sat down by the fire, and it was agreed that Detective Cardwell should tell them first about the strange death of Sir Walter Cross and the disappearance of his dachshund, Doughnut.

Outside the day grew darker and the snow turned thicker, while inside no one noticed a key slip off the armchair and quietly leave the room.

"Sir Walter Cross had been having unbelievably good luck on the horses," said Detective Cardwell. "He had developed an extraordinary knack of choosing the winner in every race."

"How did he choose the winners?" asked Emily.

"That's a question many people would like to know the answer to," said Detective Cardwell. "I have my suspicions. Sir Walter swore he used mathematics, that it was only a matter of understanding the numbers. But I don't believe a word of it. There's more here than can be seen by a human eye. I'm sure Sir Walter was being helped by someone; someone in the fairy realm. Then again, I have never known a fairy to be in debt to a human being. Usually it's the other way 'round." Detective Cardwell stood up and walked back and forth. "But a fairy is only allowed to grant three wishes to any one person."

"Why?" asked Emily. "Why only three?"

"This is what I mean," said Buster. "It's impossible working with humans. They ask the stupidest questions."

"It just isn't done," said James Cardwell. "Can you imagine the mess if fairies granted them willy-nilly?"

"Mr. Rollo made more than three wishes, and his luck turned to fish bones," said Fidget.

Emily and Buster turned and looked at Fidget.

"Mr. Rollo?"

"Mr. Rollo, the tailor who came to see me today," said Fidget. "His luck has gone fish-belly-up and rather smelly, if you get my drift."

"Not really," said Emily.

"That's the case I took on."

"I don't understand," said Emily.

"We are investigating where his good luck went and why all his wishes came true and then turned bad," said Fidget.

Detective Cardwell's phone bleeped.

"Buddleia," he said, reading a text. "I've been called back to Scotland Yard. I think you should start with Sir Walter Cross—after all, the gentleman was murdered." He put on his hat and coat. "I'll have to leave the case to you to investigate. Are you up to it?"

"Yes," said Emily firmly.

"Of course we are," said Buster. "This is Wings & Co."

Chapter Five

rs. Pauline Smith was propped up in her big brass bed, her face covered thickly with green revitalizing cream. Tomorrow her only daughter, Pandora, would finally be married. Pauline went over all the arrangements for the next day. Every little detail had been thought about, worried over, and worked out. Pan was very fussy. The church had to be just right, the tent had to be large enough for a huge sit-down dinner, and as for the wedding dress—it had been altered so many times, caused so many tears, that in the end, they had had to tell Mr. Rollo that his work wasn't up to scratch. He had lost his magic with a needle, and the design, well, it had made Pan look like a marshmallow on a stick. All very embarrassing, thought Pauline. Only last week had they bought the perfect dress from Selfridges, at vast expense to the family fortunes. She comforted herself by saying it was all worth it. Pan had been on a miracle diet, and almost overnight, her skin, not her best feature, was blemish free. Her hair, which had always been thin and mousy, was now thick and glossy. It was amazing what self-discipline and a little exercise could do.

Harry Smith lay next to his wife, counting pound coins, all of which were flying out of his wallet. Weddings were terribly expensive. Thank goodness they only had the one girl. A pity, he thought, that Pan had chosen to marry a man with the surname Pots instead of her childhood sweetheart, Derek Lowe. Harry was fond of Derek. They both supported the same soccer team.

"Pan Pots," he said sleepily to himself. "It doesn't sound right. It sounds plain daft."

As for the bride herself, she was fast asleep down the hall from her parents, her wedding dress hanging on the wardrobe door. Tomorrow all her wishes would come true. Pan's dreams were full of flowers and Happily-Ever-Afters.

It was well past midnight, and the Smith family were now so fast asleep that none of them heard the window on the ground floor being forced open. Neither did they hear the patter of small feet on the parquet floor.

The two crooks were both on the smallish side. One was called Toff the Terrible, and the other, Elvis. Elvis had elfin features and was on the whole more delicately built than his mate, who was chubby and had a furious face with bushy blue eyebrows. Toff was definitely a goblin.

"Right house?" said Toff the Terrible.

"Yes," replied Elvis, nervously. "I'm not sure— perhaps we should leave it."

"Look, you sniveling elf," said Toff, "you asked for our help, and you need our help, and you are in this deep—"

"But remember what happened last time . . ."

"Just get on with it," said Toff. "We haven't got time for your airy-fairy ways."

Toff the Terrible pushed Elvis toward the dining room. There, on a long table covered in a white linen cloth, sat the wedding cake. It was beautifully iced and surrounded by golden plates, silver candlesticks, and bowls of roses.

"It's a pity we aren't doing a robbery," said Toff. "I'd have those candlesticks."

"No," said Elvis. "That's not what we agreed—"

"Come on," said Toff. "We haven't got all night. What's first?"

"Oh dear, I'm not sure."

"You don't want me to lose my temper, now, do you? Remember what happens when I lose my temper."

Elvis remembered all too well. He peered uneasily through the French windows into the garden. The snow was still falling, and the tent looked picture-perfect for a winter wedding.

"Better get cracking here, I suppose," said Elvis.

"Oh, goody gumdrops," said Toff, and disappeared.

All that could be seen of him were sparks of light,

as if a top was spinning very fast around the room. Then it was done.

"I enjoyed that," said Toff, his mouth stuffed full of wedding cake.

Elvis took out a red notebook and looked through it unhappily before licking his pencil and marking a page.

He placed the pencil behind his pointy ear and said, "You wait here. I'll do upstairs."

Toff the Terrible lifted Elvis off his feet.

"If you want to see it again," he said, "make sure you do."

Elvis floated up the stairs and along the corridor to where the bride-to-be lay snoring. Yes, unfortunately, this was the right room and the right girl. He could tell from her cascading golden hair, so thick and plentiful. He twitched his nose, then, taking his pencil from behind his ear again, crossed out something in his notebook before turning his attention to the wedding dress.

A few minutes later, he rejoined his companion, who had by now eaten most of the wedding cake and was busy munching up the flowers.

"Roses are very tasty," Toff said. "Done?"

Elvis nodded.

And with that, the pair vanished into the night.

The morning of the wedding dawned bright and beautiful. Pan Smith, soon to be Pan Pots, woke up, rose sleepily from her bed, and went to admire herself in the mirror. At almost the same time, Pauline Smith opened the curtains to admire the tent and Harry Smith opened the dining room door to admire the wedding cake. Their joint screams could be heard all the way to the end of Mountview Drive.

Chapter Six

There was a CLOSED sign on the shop door the following day. After all, there was now more than enough work for the three of them.

Emily couldn't wait to start. In her book on how to be a detective, she had read that you needed to be able to make decisions, to listen, to pay attention, and to have a good sense of justice. But most important of all, you needed great dedication to the case at hand. After managing to defeat Harpella, the scariest witch of all time, Emily knew she was up to the job. The only trouble was Buster. Emily trudged upstairs again.

She had tried all morning to make Buster leave the warmth of the living room and start the investigation. He was on the sofa, reading a comic. Fidget had put on his overcoat and was ready to go, but now he was knitting, a hobby he had taken up recently. Every pattern Fidget attempted ended up in the shape of a fish.

"Cast one, purl one," said Fidget to himself.

"What does that mean?" asked Emily.

"I'm knitting you a sweater, my little ducks."

"Listen, we shouldn't just be sitting here," said Emily. "We should be investigating the crime scene."

"I'm as ready as catnip," said Fidget, putting down his knitting.

"Have you looked outside?" said Buster, still glued to his comic.

Emily pressed her face against the bottle-glass window. The alleyway where the shop stood was covered in a thick blanket of untrodden snow.

"A bit of bad weather shouldn't stop—" She was interrupted by a humongous noise, as if something had exploded in the shop below. The whole building wobbled, the lights flickered, the windows rattled, and smoke rushed back down the chimney and filled the room. "Oh, Fidget," she said in alarm, "is Harpella back?"

"Not possible, my little ducks," said Fidget, desperately holding on to his knitting and a plate of fish paste sandwiches.

"No one panic," said Buster, who was panicking. "The last time anyone saw the old witch, she was a purple bunny rabbit, remember? It will take her hundreds of years to get out of that pickle."

The noise seemed to be slowly climbing the stairs toward them. *Bump-bang-bump.* It sounded not unlike a dragon, hissing and snorting. The detectives were frozen to the spot like three fish sticks.

Then they heard a cell phone ring and a voice say, "Sorry, deary, I got cut off. I can't talk now, Pauline. I'm in a predicament."

"Oh, no," said Buster. "It's not . . ."

"It is," said Fidget.

"Is who?" asked Emily.

"The keys must have opened another drawer," said Buster and dashed to hide behind the sofa. "I thought it was your job to keep an eye on them," he hissed at Emily.

Emily felt this day wasn't working out as she had expected. Yes, one of the keys was missing. It was all very annoying. She was sure this didn't happen to proper detectives.

The door to the living room burst open, and there stood a fairy with a tea trolley.

"This is most inconvenient, deary, most inconvenient indeed," she said to Fidget. "Pauline rang me just before I started my tea round and then . . . you could have given me some warning."

"Hello, Lettice. Good to see you, my old cod."

"Where am I?" asked Lettice.

"In Podgy Bottom, in the shop. Remember? You handed in your wings for safekeeping," said Fidget.

"But that was a hundred years ago. I've moved on since then. Wings are most unsuitable for modern living. Anyway, no one takes fairies seriously these days.

Have you seen what they have done to us in the media? We are pink and silly—not like the old times, when fairies were given the respect and loathing they deserved."

Emily looked on, wonderstruck. Lettice was round, with a nose like the beak of a bird. She had a cheerful face, tied her gray hair back in a ponytail, and wore an apron over her trousers and top. Apart from her wings, she didn't look one bit like a fairy.

"What's with the tea trolley, dear old trout?" asked Fidget.

"I was about to hand the prime minister a gingersnap," said Lettice, "when I was whizzed back here."

"The prime minister?" said Emily.

"Yes, deary. I work as a tea lady in the Houses of Parliament. One could say, deary, that without me the country would go to custard creams."

At that moment, the magic lamp came into the living room, followed by a bashful-looking key. When Lettice saw the lamp, she screamed and stood on a chair, her wings flapping.

"What's that thing doing here?"

Since the lamp had worked for the witch Harpella, it had turned over a new gold leaf.

"Excuse me," it said, offended. "I am now shining with good intentions. I helped a key to open your drawer. I nobly allowed it to stand on my lid. And this is all the thanks I receive."

"It's quite harmless," explained Emily. "Ever since I removed the dragon's tooth."

"No, deary, I'm sorry, but a lamp like that can be a dangerous thing if it falls into the wrong hands. I mean, deary, you never know what magic could be stuffed inside it. And you are . . . ?"

"Emily Vole."

"Not the famous Emily Vole?" said Lettice. "Savior of the fairies?" Carefully she climbed down from the chair and straightened her apron. "So brave. Such a brave girl. A pleasure to meet you at last, deary, a pleasure, I'm sure." She turned and sniffed, and sniffed again. "I see you've not learned any manners yet," she said, pulling Buster out from behind the sofa by the ear. "One hundred years of being eleven, and no improvement. Haven't you got a kiss for your Auntie Lettice?"

"Auntie?" said Emily, surprised that Buster had an auntie.

"Yes," replied Buster. "This is my aunt, Lettice Lovage."

Lettice sat down on the sofa. "Pour us a cuppa from the tea trolley, there's a love," she said. "I'm all at sixes and sevens."

To Emily's amaze- ment, Buster did as he was told.

Lettice's cell phone rang again.

"Pauline, I'm sorry, something just sprang up, so to speak." Lettice listened for a minute. "Well, as it happens, deary, I'm in Podgy Bottom. Wait a mo." She turned to Fidget. "How long would it take to get to Mountview Drive?"

"Not long, as the crow flies," said Fidget.

"I'm not a crow," said Lettice.

"You are a fairy," Buster reminded her. "And you have your wings back, which is more than I do."

"Pauline, deary, what number? Twenty-two. . . . Hang on, I can be there in no time. Are the police there now? Yes . . . and a doctor? Don't panic, Pauline. Keep breathing. I'll be with you shortly."

"Wait," said Emily, as Lettice stood up to leave. "What's happened? Who's Pauline?"

"I can't stop, deary. Fidget, I'm parking my tea trolley here. Now, handbag . . . cell phone . . . wings."

And with that, Lettice Lovage was gone.

Chapter Seven

The keys and the magic lamp had scampered down the stairs after Lettice. Emily followed hastily and found them dancing around in front of the curious cabinets, giggling. She couldn't see what they found so funny. She wasn't even sure that the keys could giggle.

"What's the joke?" she asked the magic lamp.

"We are celebrating," replied the lamp. "It is a big day when a key opens one of the drawers."

Emily crouched so that she was on the same level as the keys.

"You don't feel like opening any more drawers, do you?" she asked hopefully. The keys all stopped jumping up and down and turned to face her. "Think of all those fairies who long to have their wings back. Especially Buster."

The keys looked as solemn as only ironmongery can.

"No," said the magic lamp, who had become spokesperson for the keys. "It doesn't work like that. I thought you, Emily Vole, of all people, would understand."

"But I don't," said Emily. "It's simple. They just need to open the drawers. That's what keys do. Open things."

There was an uncomfortable silence, then, with an air of injured pride, the magic lamp, followed by a single file of keys, walked back up the stairs.

Emily stared out of the shop window and thought to herself that being Keeper of the Keys wasn't all it was cracked up to be. She was just about to join the others when she saw a small dog. It was making leaps in the snow in an effort to reach the shop door. Emily went outside. The little fellow had huge chunks of snow frozen to his fur. She lifted him up and brushed him down. His name tag read DOUGHNUT. Emily ran back inside and up the stairs to the living room, clutching the first break-through in the murder of Sir Walter Cross.

"Look who I've found," she said.

"If it's another aunt, I don't want to know," said Buster, his nose still in a comic.

"It's Doughnut," said Emily, taking the poor frozen hound to the fire and plopping him down on the rug.

The second that Doughnut saw Fidget, he started to bark as if his life depended on it.

"Oh, for goodness' sake! Quiet, Bonzo," said Buster.

"Woff. Gree-ahhhh woof," said Fidget.

Doughnut stopped in mid-bark.

Emily and Buster looked at Fidget.

"You speak Dog?" said Buster.

"Only a smattering," said Fidget modestly. "All cats have to have the basics. It comes with the Nine Lives package."

"What did you say to him?" asked Emily.

"Put a fishbone in it."

"Can he tell us what happened to Sir Walter Cross?"

At the mention of his master's name, Doughnut was up on all fours, tail wagging, nose pointed. He stared at

the living room door, head on one side, as if he expected his master to walk through it at any minute.

"Sir Walter's not coming back," said Emily, and tried to comfort him.

"He won't understand," said Buster. "You don't speak Dog."

Doughnut looked at Buster, and Emily was certain that she saw a glint in the dog's eye. A not-altogether-friendly glint.

Then the little chap jumped into the air, landed on the carpet, and rolled over dead.

"Oh no," said Emily, bending over him. Doughnut was lying on his side, his whole body stiff, his paws outstretched. "You don't think he's died of cold?"

"No, my little ducks," said Fidget. "I think he is trying to tell us something."

At that, Doughnut sprang to life and did the whole show over again, this time with an added woof as he jumped up in the air.

"I bet it's to do with how Sir Walter died," said Emily. "Fidget, just how much Dog do you speak?"

"I can say 'go away, or I will scratch your eyes out,'

and 'do you really want to fight a furious cat with claws?' and 'put a fishbone in it.' That's all the Dog I know, apart from having a natural caution regarding the canine race itself."

"That doesn't help much," said Emily. "But you're right. He's trying to tell us something. I read in one of my books that important witnesses are put into protection programs. That's what we need to do. Doughnut knows who the murderer is."

"Humans," sighed Buster. "They think they understand dogs, and they don't."

Doughnut growled at him.

Emily picked up the little chap and stroked him.

"He seems to understand you very well indeed," she said.

"There is one person I know who can speak Dog," said Fidget, putting down his knitting. "And that, Buster, is your Aunt Lettice."

"No!" said Buster. "Anyone but my aunt, please. I mean—isn't there a book on the subject?"

"I doubt it," said Emily. "Anyway, why would we need one when your aunt speaks Dog?"

"You don't understand," said Buster. "Believe me, it isn't worth asking her. She has a fearful temper and—"

"Twenty-two Mountview Drive, I think," interrupted Fidget, standing up.

"Doughnut can't go out in the cold again," said Emily.

Fidget pulled one of his early fish knits from his knitting basket. It had turned out to be far too small for Emily, but it fit Doughnut perfectly. His head stuck out of the fish's mouth.

"Look, it's not a good idea," said Buster. "Can't we leave Aunt Lettice out of this?"

But Emily, Fidget, and Doughnut were already halfway down the stairs.

Chapter Eight

They arrived at Mountview Drive just as the police were leaving. Fidget rang the bell. The front door was opened by Lettice Lovage, her wings well hidden by a thick knit cardigan.

"What are you doing here, Fidget?" she asked.

"Hello again, Lettice, my old cod," replied Fidget. "Nice cardigan."

"We need help, Aunt Lettice. Do you speak Dog?" said Buster, who couldn't bear to be left out, aunts or no aunts.

"I don't have time for this, deary. We have a catastrophe here."

"If you could just translate a bit of Dog for us," said

Buster, walking into the hall uninvited, "we would be out of your hair."

To Emily's surprise, Lettice grasped him by the ear and led him to the door. "Go home, you little squirt," she said.

"That's not a nice way to talk to your nephew," said Buster, wriggling to free himself.

"You are not a nice nephew. Never once in a hundred years did you bother to see how your Auntie Lettice was doing, and now, when I'm in the middle of a catastrophe, you ask me if I speak Dog."

She looked down to see Doughnut's brown eyes staring up at her.

"I am sorry," said Emily. "We didn't mean to come barging in at a bad time, but we do need your help rather urgently."

"Oh, buddleia," said Lettice, letting go of Buster's ear. "Catastrophes are like buses. There are always at least two at once. You'd better come in."

They were standing awkwardly in the hall, Buster nursing his injured pride and a sore ear, when a door opened. A woman poked her head out.

"It's not the press, is it, Lettice?" she asked.

"No, Pauline. Don't worry, deary. I'll be with you in a mo, just as soon as I've made the tea."

The door closed again.

"You will have to wait in here until I have a minute to deal with this," said Lettice, taking them into the dining room. "Don't touch a thing," she added as she left.

"See?" said Buster. "I told you. A book or some such thing would be more useful any day than my old aunt."

Emily took no notice. She looked around the room.

It was a complete mess. There were broken plates, bits of wedding cake, flowers, and glasses strewn all over the floor, and through the French windows, she could see that in the garden a tent had been torn to ribbons.

"Pickle me a herring," said Fidget. "This takes some beating."

"Probably Aunt Lettice blew a fuse," said Buster

helpfully. "She has quite a temper. Look what she did to my ear."

"I wonder what happened," said Emily.

"I'm telling you what happened," said Buster.

Emily stuck her head out into the hall. She could hear someone sobbing upstairs.

"I'm going to find out," she said. "Something odd is going on."

"That's not a good idea," said Buster. "If Aunt Lettice can do this to a dining room and a tent, think what she will do when she finds you have gone off exploring."

"Don't be silly," said Emily. "Your aunt had nothing to do with this—did she, Fidget?"

"No, of course not," agreed Fidget. "This looks as serious as a cat without whiskers."

Emily, followed by Doughnut, left the others in the wrecked dining room and crept up the stairs to where the sound of sobbing could be heard in one of the rooms. She knocked on the door.

"Go away," said a voice.

Emily knocked again.

"You don't know me, but I'm very good at listening," she said. "And I have a small dog."

Emily was banking on the dog bit being a winner. After all, nearly everyone liked animals. They had furry ears, good for listening to problems. She waited for what felt like ages before finally she heard the lock turn.

Gingerly, Emily went in. There, sitting on the tiles next to the bath, her face all blotchy red, was a chubby young woman. In her hand she held a photo. Doughnut rushed up to her and gave her a good lick.

"I'm Emily Vole, and this is Doughnut."

The young woman said nothing, but burst into tears again and buried her face in Doughnut's fish knit coat. The photo fell to the floor.

Emily picked it up and studied it carefully. It showed a young couple, both wearing tracksuits. On the girl's top was the name PAN in diamanté studs. She had thick blond hair and a fit figure. The man, whose name was not on his tracksuit, was tall, suntanned, and handsome. And rather pleased with himself. To Emily's way of thinking, there was something fake about the two of them. Pan looked more like a doll than a real, living human being.

Emily tried to work out what this picture might have to do with the young woman weeping on the bathroom floor.

"What's your name?" Emily asked her.

"Pan," sobbed the young woman. "And that is a picture of me and my fiancé. It was taken last week. We were to be married today."

Chapter Nine

Pan wiped her eyes and said, "You don't believe me, do you?"

Emily, who always thought honesty was the best policy, said, "No."

Pan's wail went up the musical scale.

"What I mean," said Emily, above the din, "is that the woman in the photo looks like a plastic doll. Whereas you look lovely. That is, you would if your face wasn't all red and blotchy."

"But look at my hair and my figure," howled Pan. "I was beautiful. Now Kyle won't marry me."

Doughnut looked dolefully up into her face.

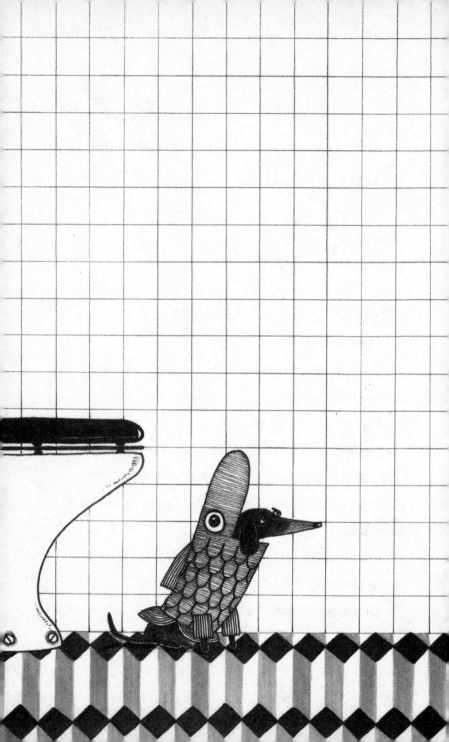

"Are you sure?" asked Emily.

"Yes," sniffed Pan. "He came 'round this morning, and the minute he saw me, he said he had been tricked."

"What does Kyle do?" asked Emily, certain that this was the kind of question a detective should ask.

"He works for his father's company. It makes false teeth."

Emily thought that must explain his dreadful smile.

"Mummy was really pleased that I was marrying into such a posh family. Kyle's parents own a Bentley and a Rolls-Royce. Mr. Pots said he would make Daddy a member of his golf club."

"Pots?" interrupted Emily. "You could never marry a man called Pots. Pan Pots sounds silly."

Pan started to cry all over again. Emily, being a practical girl and quite used to the high drama of her ex-adoptive-mother-slash-employer, Daisy Dashwood, found a washcloth. She told Pan no quantity of tears would solve the problem and to wipe her face and stop crying.

To Emily's relief, Pan did both.

"Much better," said Emily. "Now, please begin at the beginning so that I can write down all the facts."

She took out her notepad, one of the main things you needed if you were ever to be a proper detective.

"If I tell you, you'll think that I'm making it up," said Pan.

"Why would I think that?"

"I tried to tell Mummy, but she refused to believe me. She said she knew my secret—that I'd had a face-lift, a nose job, liposuction, and a hair graft. But I hadn't."

Emily suddenly remembered what James Cardwell had said about wishes and the mess they create if they are handed out willy-nilly. A light went on in her brain.

"Did you make a wish?" she asked.

"That's amazing," said Pan. "How did you know?"

"Because I'm from Wings & Co., the fairy detective agency," explained Emily.

"Never!" said Pan. "Get away with you. Are you for real?"

"Yes," said Emily.

"Wow. That's impressive," said Pan. She paused. "I made several wishes, if you must know."

"I must," said Emily. "Carry on."

Pan had been engaged for two years to Sir Walter Cross's gardener, Derek Lowe.

"Sir Walter Cross?" said Emily. "That's interesting."

It had all started on Derek's birthday last year. Pan had surprised him at work with a picnic lunch and bubbles. Emily wasn't sure what bubbles were, but as Pan was in full flow, she thought it might be a mistake to ask. They had finished lunch, and Derek had gone back to work. Pan was about to walk home when, under the willow tree by the duck pond, a small gentleman popped up. He asked her, if she could have one wish, what would it be?

That morning she had been flicking through a hair magazine, and in one of the articles, it said that the plainest girl could be transformed by beautiful hair. Pan said the first thing that came into her head.

The next morning, she had golden locks. Derek, on seeing his beloved, was upset. He wanted to know what she had done. Her hair looked all wrong. Pan didn't care. She was thrilled. When the little gentleman came to see if she was pleased with her hair, she said she would be, if only she had a slim, toned figure to go with it.

When Derek saw her new shape, he was even more distressed. Where, he wondered, had all her lovely curves gone? Was she ill? Pan asked him if he wasn't delighted to see the new woman she had become. He said all he wanted was his sweet Pan back the way she had always been.

Shortly after that, she met Kyle, and it was love at first sight. Kyle thought her perfect in every way. She called off her engagement to Derek Lowe and, a month later, was engaged to be married to Kyle Pots.

The small gentleman came again, and determined to make the most of her good fortune, Pan had a list ready this time. It included perfect teeth, smaller or larger boobs—Emily couldn't work out which way around that went—the perfect wedding dress, a tent, money forever, a car—no, three cars . . . Pan's face began to crumble.

"We were going on a golfing honeymoon."

"Do you like golf?" asked Emily.

Pan stopped mid-sob.

"No, not really," she said. "But Mummy said that's what people with good pensions do—play golf—and it showed Kyle would be able to look after me right into Happily-Ever-After."

"I suppose so," said Emily. "As long as you stayed stick-thin, with thick blond hair and perfect teeth."

"You're right," said Pan. "I hadn't thought of that, but then again, I did have all my wishes come true, so I believed it would just carry on."

"Can you give me a description of the little gentleman?" said Emily, knowing that was the kind of question a good detective should ask.

"He was small and—oh, I don't know . . ." said Pan.

"Anything at all would help."

"He was . . . brightly colored. He looked like an exploded paint pot."

Chapter Ten

Buster was in one big grump when he walked into the kitchen at Mountview Drive. Or more to the point, when he discovered the fridge. There on a shelf, all lit up in a cut-glass bowl, was a trifle. On the top the words PAN & KYLE were carefully written in icing, surrounded by tiny strawberries.

What harm could there be, thought Buster, *to have just one strawberry?* No one would notice one strawberry was missing. He was rather peckish.

There was something about the taste of that strawberry when it was snowing outside that made him think of the summer to come. Buster couldn't resist taking another one. The trifle still looked all right. He thought it might even look better if he ate all the strawberries.

He munched away, lost in thought, and this is what he thought: that as much as he didn't like Emily Vole—which was quite a lot, and maybe more than a lot—there was no getting away from the fact that she was a good detective.

"Buddleia," said Buster, taking the trifle from the fridge and rummaging in a drawer for a spoon. If only she was terrible at the job, that would make it better. He had followed her upstairs and listened at the bathroom door. She was asking Pan Smith all the right kinds of questions.

"Buddleia," said Buster again, out loud. "Buddleia!"

And without thinking about it, which later he realized was a mistake, he put his finger through the iced words so that PAN & KYLE was nothing more than a wiggly mess of custard and cream.

That's done it, thought Buster. *But perhaps if I eat the whole thing and wash up the bowl, no one will notice it's missing.*

He dug his spoon through the thick layers of cream, custard, cake, and jelly. Mmm. It was very good. Not too runny, all firm and delicious.

Comforted by the taste of trifle, he went through his list of complaints. Number one was that Miss String had left Wings & Co. to Emily Vole. Two, Emily was a girl. Three, she wasn't even a fairy. Four—well, four was four.

It didn't seem fair. After all, Miss String hadn't known Emily that long. If anyone should have been left the shop, it should have been his friend James Cardwell. Buster thought back sadly to those glory days when he and Jimmy had been eleven and twelve, and master sleuths. No crime had been too big or too small for their fairy talent. Now James was all grown up and Buster was still eleven. It hurt, if he thought about it. Actually, it hurt quite a lot.

He sighed and took another spoonful of trifle.

But he had to admit to himself that it wasn't Emily's fault. Neither was the fact that Fidget was so fond of

her. After all, he, Buster, hadn't been exactly nice to anyone. He looked down at the bowl, half emptied of trifle.

Oh, heck! Who was he trying to fool? Of course Miss String had known what she was doing. The minute the keys had chosen Emily, the shop would have to be hers. It followed as night followed day. There was no denying it. In all the ninety years he had known Miss String, the keys had never taken a shine to him. Miss String had often said how sad she was about it.

Maybe, thought Buster, putting another huge spoonful of trifle in his mouth, *maybe it was my fault. I shouldn't have kept tying their boot laces together. Oh, I have to snap out of this. It doesn't suit a detective of my skills. I am being a right chump. Here are two—no, three—good cases to solve, and all I can do is sulk.*

He ate another spoonful and finally admitted to himself that he was trying to fill a hole that no amount of trifle could fill. If he was truthful, he had to admit Emily Vole was pretty amazing.

By now there wasn't a scrap of trifle left in the bowl. He was about to wash it up and go back and join Fidget when he nearly jumped out of his socks. Lettice was calling his name.

He rushed to the sink but unfortunately slipped on some trifle he'd dropped on the shiny floor. It was then that the bowl and Buster parted company. The bowl went one way and smashed to the ground in a hundred tiny pieces as Buster went the other way, slipped backward, and bumped his head on the stove.

For a moment, he saw stars, and when the stars had cleared, standing above him, hands on hips, was his Aunt Lettice, looking none too pleased. In fact, looking mighty furious.

Behind her, Pauline Smith screamed at the top of her voice, "How could you? How could you eat the only thing that wasn't destroyed?"

Seeing so much rage staring down at him, Buster knew "sorry" wasn't going to work.

"Oh, buddleia," he said.

Chapter Eleven

On the edge of the woods, not far from where Sir Walter Cross had lived, there was a large oak tree. It was agreed by the locals that the area surrounding the tree was best avoided at night. Anyone going that way was asking for trouble.

Which was true. For this was the home of Toff the Terrible and his Band of Baddies. It was hidden deep beneath the roots of the tree. Here they slept all day and caused havoc at night. Toff the Terrible had never liked humans. He didn't trust them as far as he could throw them—which was a surprisingly long way. He thought on the whole they were selfish, greedy, vain, and given to making wishes like there was no tomorrow.

"Wishes-dishes," said Toff, as he lay tucked up in his bed, surrounded by huge piles of chocolates and sweets. That stupid Elvis had handed out wishes to anyone who asked for them, and some who hadn't. It wasn't right. It had to be stopped. Humans had enough going for them as it was without having their every mealymouthed wish granted. He had enjoyed making the elf punish the tailor, that silly girl, and the greedy old man. And, even better, now he had Elvis the Elf's umbrella. He was halfway to becoming the most powerful goblin that had ever bossed the world around. He only needed a magic lamp and, thanks to a news item he had recently read in an old copy of the magazine *Fairy World International*, he knew where to find one. Toff yawned. Come the dark, he would have the magic lamp too. And with that happy thought skipping across his mind, Toff the Terrible fell fast asleep.

In a dormitory down the long, winding passage, Toff's

Band of Baddies were also tucked up in their beds, snug as bugs in rugs. In the guest room, Elvis the Elf was wide awake.

He couldn't sleep, not during the day. It felt all wrong. Everything felt all wrong. Oh, dear, what had he done? He should have kept quiet about the wishes. He rather wished he had. Elvis felt a shiver of deep regret, remembering what had happened to Sir Walter Cross. Oh, what a mess, what a terrible mess. As for Doughnut . . . at least he'd saved him from Sir Walter's fate, and if only that dear little creature hadn't run away, he would have looked after him. Elvis needed a friend. But now it was too late.

He had been a fool to ask Toff the Terrible for help. Elvis hadn't wanted to punish the humans for their greed, but Toff had insisted that it was part of the deal. Elvis had to agree, for what was he meant to do without his spotty red and white umbrella, his only means of transport?

Without that umbrella, he was unable to go home to his mum and dad. It didn't matter how many wishes Elvis had granted Sir Walter Cross, the man had refused to give it back. Now Toff the Terrible had it, and he wouldn't give it back either. Elvis didn't know why.

"Oh, what a mess," said Elvis to himself.

The goblins' house was a mess too.

Like many elves, Elvis was very tidy and took great pride in his appearance. He was used to things being just so, not like the goblins, who had no manners whatsoever. They dunked their cookies in tea, threw food onto the floor, fired spitballs at one another, and, worst of all, held farting competitions. It was all too much for a sensitive elf. Elvis decided then and there he wouldn't stay a moment longer. He would escape, and umbrella or no umbrella, he'd tidy up the mess he'd made as best he could.

He took his suitcase from under the bed and neatly packed his socks and vests and his new red tweed coat, still wrapped in tissue paper. He put on his orange coat and his bright green hat, wrapped a long purple scarf around his delicate throat, and quietly closed the guest room door behind him. He crept like a mouse in velvet slippers down the long corridor past Toff the Terrible's quarters. He could hear Toff snoring, an awful sound that shook the roots of the old tree. On he went into the Great Hall. Slumped by the front door, surrounded by half-eaten chocolate cookies, were two goblin guards, asleep on duty. This was the tricky part. Elvis balanced the suitcase on his head and trod daintily between the tangle of legs. Now all he had to do was unbolt the door, and he would be free. The door creaked open, and to Elvis's relief, the goblin guards snored on. Outside the snow fell. It was much deeper than Elvis had thought, and he tripped. A branch snapped. Underneath him a wire pinged, and a bell started ringing.

The front door burst open, and there stood two furious-looking goblin guards. Elvis scrambled to his feet and took hold of his suitcase.

"Where do you think you're going?" asked one of them.

Elvis felt his tummy turn to jelly.

"Oh, just out to take some air," said Elvis, backing away.

The goblin chuckled. "You think you can escape us? Well, think again."

Elvis turned and ran as fast as his little legs would carry him.

The goblin guards chased him for a while but soon gave up. All the chocolate had made them stout, and they ran out of puff quickly. Elvis was now out of reach.

"I will have you roasted for this!" one shouted after him.

What a mess, thought Elvis. *Oh, dear, what a mess.*

Chapter Twelve

It had stopped snowing by the time Emily, Buster, and Fidget reached the alleyway that led to Wings & Co. Emily, who was carrying Doughnut, was not in a good mood. Neither, for that matter, was Fidget.

"It wasn't my fault we got kicked out of Mountview Drive," said Buster resentfully.

"It was," said Emily. "It most definitely was."

"No," said Buster firmly. "I was only doing what all good detectives do."

"What's that?" asked Fidget.

"I was thinking," said Buster.

"Oh," sighed Emily, "give me strength."

"If you hadn't gone wandering off and asking

questions," Buster said, "we would still be there. I told you Aunt Lettice had a temper."

"At least I found out something," said Emily, opening the shop door. "And I would have found out a whole lot more if it wasn't for you. I'm sure the crime at Mountview Drive is connected to our cases."

"It's a lot of fuss over a trifle," said Buster.

"Put a fishbone in it," said Fidget. "If you had stayed put, we might now know what Doughnut has to say. We might even know who murdered Sir Walter."

"Look," said Buster, who was fed up with everyone attacking him, "I hadn't eaten anything all day."

"Oh, whatever," said Emily, who was so cross that she thought it was hardly worth talking to him at all.

Inside they were greeted by the magic lamp.

"At last!" it said. "There's a right how's-your-genie going on upstairs. I can't find the living room, and the keys are locked in."

"That's all we need," said Fidget. "Even the shop has taken umbrage."

"Taken what?" said Buster.

"Umbrage," said Emily, putting Doughnut down. "It means it's taken offense. In other words, it's as cross with you as I am."

"It might just be having an off day," said Buster.

"I doubt it," said Fidget. "Unless . . ." He stopped, his whiskers twitching.

The building had been designed many moons ago by a magician. It was, as Emily knew all too well, unlike any other shop. For a start, it was built on four iron legs with griffin's talons, and when the fancy took it, the shop could get up and walk away. It also had a rather annoying habit of moving the upstairs rooms around, although Emily had thought that recently this particular problem had settled down. She was about to go and see if she could sort it out when Fidget stopped her.

"Wait, my little ducks," said Fidget. "I think someone has broken in."

"A burglar, you mean?" said Emily.

"Spot on the fishcake, my little ducks. The shop is in lockdown."

"I can't take it," said the lamp. "It's all too much for me. Do you think Harpella—"

"Pull yourself together," said Fidget. "Where's your mettle?"

"I'm an empty lamp," it said. "Any old genie or dragon's tooth could get inside me. Then where would I be? Lost, lost, I tell you!"

"How irritating you are," Buster.

"Not as irritating as you," said Emily, picking up the lamp.

"Sweet mistress," said the lamp. "Thank you."

Doughnut started to growl, his tail out straight, his nose sniffing the air. He stood at the foot of the stairs and barked loudly. Emily was about to call him when there was a noise of something or somebody whirling down the stairs toward them at great speed.

"Scary," is what Emily remembered.

"Hairy," is how Buster described it.

"Fishy," is what Fidget had to say.

In a flash of red smoke, it was gone, leaving behind a smell of farts and a broken front door.

Doughnut and the magic lamp were nowhere to be seen.

Chapter Thirteen

Mr. Rollo, the tailor, was in his shop studying his account books. Nothing added up. It was hard to believe that everything had gone so terribly wrong. Three days ago, his wife had moved back to her mum's. Rosalind couldn't cope with the damp in the house. The carpets were already soggy. It was enough to make the tailor cry. He was about as low as the lowest branch of a weeping willow. When the shop bell rang, he looked around for his glasses, but they, like everything else, had vanished. Unable to see properly, he went to explain that he was closed, but when he opened the door, all he could make out was an explosion of colors—green, orange, and purple—somewhere near his knees.

"Yes?" said the tailor to this blurred vision. "How can I help you?"

"Can I come in?" asked the visitor. "There is something I need to talk to you about."

Mr. Rollo didn't like to be unfriendly, but he wasn't in the mood for a chat.

"Well, not now, if you don't mind."

"But I do," said the visitor. "Do you remember me?"

"I don't think so," said Mr. Rollo. "Well, it's hard to tell. I am, at the moment, well, as blind as a wombat. Are you from the theater?"

"No," said Elvis. "Are you sure that you don't remember me?"

"Should I?" asked Mr. Rollo.

Elvis felt a great weight had been lifted from him. If Mr. Rollo didn't recognize him, he could put things right without anyone knowing he was to blame for the mess in the first place.

"Can I offer you a cup of tea?" asked Mr. Rollo.

Elvis, who had been on the run ever since escaping the goblin den, couldn't think of anything nicer. He put down his suitcase.

While Mr. Rollo made the tea, Elvis sat in a chair and studied the empty shop. If only he could go home and forget about humans and wishes altogether. Mr. Rollo reappeared carrying a tea tray. He was wearing his glasses.

"Well," said the tailor. "There's a thing. They were on top of my head all along."

He handed Elvis a mug. Now he was able to make out who his guest was.

"Of course I remember you—Mr. Elvis Elf," said the tailor. "How could I forget? I made you a bright red tweed coat."

Elvis sank back into the chair.

"Well, well. Good days, those were," continued Mr. Rollo. "I remember I told you all that I wished for. Well, blow my socks off if my wishes didn't come true. You brought me great luck, Mr. Elf." He sighed. "Sadly, it's all gone." Then he added, "I made you a vest as a way of saying thank you. Silly, I know, but . . . well . . . I thought all that good fortune might have had something to do with you."

"Me?" said Elvis, his face going bright red. "Most definitely not."

"I didn't mean to upset you, Mr. Elf," said Mr. Rollo. He started to search his empty drawers. "I know it's here. I know it is. Here, I've found it." He handed Elvis a small item wrapped in tissue paper. "This is for you. I would have sent it, but I didn't have your address."

Elvis opened the parcel. Inside was a card on which was written in large handwriting, "Thank you, Mr. Elvis Elf, for all the luck you brought me."

"Oh dear," said Elvis. "What a mess."

"You don't like it?" asked the tailor.

"It's perfect. It's the best present ever. You were really going to thank me?"

"I was," said Mr. Rollo.

They were interrupted by a loud *rat-a-tat-tat* on the shop door.

Elvis jumped up, looking not unlike a hedgehog caught in the lights of a three-wheeled car. He was certain that it must be Toff the Terrible, come to make roast beef of him.

Instead, it was a tall, wiry man in a rather well-cut coat.

Mr. Rollo greeted him warmly.

"Mr. Gubbins, a pleasure to see you again. The coat looks, well, very fine indeed."

Mr. Gubbins cleared his throat.

"I am here on official business," he said. "Mr. Rollo, I must ask you to hand over the keys of the property and then skedaddle."

"Couldn't I just tidy up first?"

"No. I will say this again without compunction. Get out."

Mr. Rollo just managed to grab his coat before he and Elvis were kicked out onto the snowy pavement. Mr. Rollo helped Elvis to his feet.

"Are you all right?" he asked.

"No," said Elvis.

The shop door opened again, and the elf's suitcase flew out and landed at his feet, followed by the vest.

Elvis knew he had been a very foolish elf indeed.

Chapter Fourteen

Emily lay on her bed watching as the ceiling turned into a sky, all golden, with pink clouds floating past. *There's a lot to be said*, she thought, *for living above a magic shop.*

Yet something about that sky reminded Emily of airplanes. And airplanes reminded her of her mother and father. And the huge unanswered question that she often asked herself: Why had they never come back to find her?

Emily had been abandoned as a baby, left in a hatbox at Stansted Airport. The story she always told herself when feeling a touch on the blue side was this: Her mother was a princess, and her father was a Gypsy.

They had been trying to escape the fury of the king, who had never wanted his daughter to marry the Gypsy in the first place. They had made it as far as Stansted Airport, where there had been a most terrible fight with the king's men. The Gypsy, wounded in the arm, had accidentally dropped the hatbox, leaving Emily fast asleep inside with only a trick clock for company. Her parents made good their escape, caught a plane, and flew away.

The trouble was that Emily couldn't understand why they had never come back to find her. She wondered if her parents had been kidnapped in some faraway land, or taken hostage by pirates, or were prisoners in the dungeons of a goblin king, a place full of dragons that liked nothing better than to feed on the toes of humans. If that was the case, thought Emily, maybe she needed to rescue them. But how? That was the question.

The clouds on the ceiling disappeared, and in their place was a red-and-white-striped puppet theater with Mr. Punch holding a baby.

"Hello, hello," said Punch.

"Are you talking to me?" asked Emily.

"Yes, I am," said Punch. "Here, catch the baby."

It fell with a thud on Emily's bed.

"That's the way to do it," said Punch.

Emily laughed out loud as Mr. Punch's wife, Judy, appeared in the puppet theater.

"Where's my baby?" said Judy.

"Here," said Emily.

"No, it's not," said Punch.

"Yes, it is," said Emily, standing on tiptoe. Judy leaned down and took the baby back.

"Give me the baby," said Punch.

"No," said Judy. "It's my baby."

Punch grabbed hold of the baby, but Judy held on to its feet and they pulled it one way, then the other.

"That's not nice," said Emily, laughing. "Not nice at all."

Punch and Judy stopped what they were doing. Judy leaned over the side of the stage.

"Who said we were nice?" she said.

"But you have a baby," said Emily.

"That doesn't make us nice," said Judy.

And with that, the Punch and Judy show vanished and the ceiling went back to normal.

Emily sat down on the bed. It was, she thought, a good point. The princess and the Gypsy might not be at all nice. They might be even worse than her adoptive parents had been, and they were pretty terrible. What if she found them and they didn't want Emily to live with Fidget? What if they said she couldn't stay with Wings & Co.? That would be worse than anything she could imagine.

"Ah, here you are." Lettice Lovage walked into Emily's bedroom and sat next to her on the bed. "I've had a little chat with my nephew. Now, I just wanted to say, deary, you did a wonderful job with my goddaughter, Pan. No one could have done better. She came out of her room and told me that she had been a fool."

"Good," said Emily. "But that doesn't solve the mystery of who granted all those wishes."

"Quite right, deary," said Lettice. "So where's that dog you wanted me to talk to?"

"He's gone," said Emily sadly.

"What do you mean, gone, deary?"

"There was this red tornado," explained Emily. "It

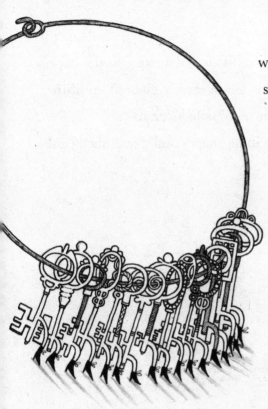

whizzed down the stairs, and the next thing we knew, Doughnut and the magic lamp had vanished."

"Never! Are the keys safe, deary?"

"Yes," said Emily. "The shop locked them in the living room and disappeared it. But what about Doughnut and the lamp?"

"Personally, deary, I was never keen on that lamp. Dogs are a different matter altogether. The dog we must find."

"Tea's ready," Fidget called up from the kitchen.

"He's been busy making cupcakes," explained Lettice, "with red and green icing. He told me they're your favorite."

Emily stood up and followed Lettice to the door. Before she left her bedroom, Emily glanced up at the ceiling again and saw Judy's silhouette there.

"Families come in all shapes and sizes," she heard the puppet say.

Chapter Fifteen

What Lettice Lovage had said to Buster, Emily was never to know, but the result was a transformation of sorts. Now here was the detective of whom James Cardwell had spoken so fondly. Buster Ignatius Spicer was on the case.

As Emily, Fidget, and he had their tea and cupcakes, Buster went over the facts. First, there was the murder of Sir Walter Cross.

"It can't have been a human who bumped him off, for no human has the power to shoot a man into the air just like that. Whoever committed the crime must be from the fairy world. Still, there seems to be no good reason why anyone would want to do away with him."

"Perhaps he made wishes, like Pan?" suggested Emily. "James thought Sir Walter was being helped by someone in the fairy realm. But there must be a reason why the fairy was so generous."

"Very good, my little ducks," said Fidget. "I hadn't thought of that."

"Not bad," agreed Buster. "Go on."

Emily was almost speechless. Could it be that Buster was taking her seriously?

"We know . . . ," said Emily, waiting for Buster to make fun of her, "we know Sir Walter had good luck on the horses and that it lasted for some time." Emily stopped, still waiting for a snide comment from Buster.

Instead, he said again, "Go on."

"Is it possible that Sir Walter had some sort of hold over the fairy?"

"A good point, my little ducks," said Fidget. "Because a fairy is only allowed to hand out three wishes to any one human, and this fairy was handing out wishes like they were nets full of fish, which is very Un-FF."

"What does that mean?" asked Emily.

"Un-Fairy-Friendly," said Buster. "There is also the matter of Doughnut. Why didn't he die in the fall? Why was he saved, only to be snatched away this morning?"

The three of them thought for a long time.

"It's all my fault that we didn't hear what Doughnut had to say," said Buster. He paused, then added in a whisper that a mouse might have had trouble hearing, "I'm sorry. Nothing like that will happen again."

Fidget and Emily glanced at each other. Fidget cleared his throat. "Pickled Herring Number Two," he said, dusting cake crumbs from his whiskers.

"Mr. Rollo was a tailor who ran a successful business in the high street. He worked for the theater, had a long waiting list of customers, and had just bought his dream house. In fact, as he told me, all his wishes had come true. Then, like an exploding salmon, everything went to fish paste. His business, fish paste; his house, fish paste. In other words, gone."

"But he is still alive," said Emily. "If it was the same

fairy who granted his wishes, why was Sir Walter Cross bumped off and not the tailor?"

"Maybe," said Buster, eating the red icing off a cupcake, "because the fairy hasn't got 'round to it yet."

"Oh dear," said Emily.

"Yes," said Buster. "Now to Case Number Three. Emily, over to you."

"There's an interesting link here to Sir Walter Cross," said Emily. "Pan Smith's ex-boyfriend was his gardener."

"Aha!" said Buster. "You're right—these cases are connected."

"Pan had all her wishes granted," continued Emily, looking at her notes. "The list includes beautiful hair, a new body, a new boyfriend, a perfect wedding dress, money, cars—it's a very long list indeed. Then, on the night before her wedding, everything was ruined." Emily stopped. "I've had a thought," she said.

"What?" said Buster and Fidget together.

"I don't think it's possible for someone who is generous enough to hand out all those wishes in the first place to be so destructive and cruel. I think there might be other fairies involved."

"I think you're right, my little ducks," said Fidget.

"So, to sum up," said Buster, "we are agreed that all three cases are related to one another?"

"Spot on the fishcake," said Fidget.

"What do you think, Emily?" asked Buster.

Emily found to her surprise that she was rather pleased that Buster wanted to know what she was thinking.

As if it didn't matter a jot, she said, "There are a lot of unanswered questions. Two of them are: Who was it we saw on the stairs, and why did they take Doughnut and the magic lamp?"

The phone rang, and Fidget answered it.

"Wings & Co.," he said. "Fairy Detective Agency."

At last, Emily thought, *we are real detectives.*

"That sounds like more fairy meddling, my old mackerel. Keep us in the net." Fidget put down the phone. "That was Jimmy Cardwell. Mr. Rollo the tailor has been arrested."

"Why?" said Emily.

"He was discovered on Podgy Bottom High Street in possession of five bags of gold."

Chapter Sixteen

Elvis the Elf was feeling very pleased with himself indeed. He'd had a brilliant idea and had righted one wrong. It was nothing short of fairy wizardry to give Mr. Rollo five large sacks of gold coins. They would solve all the tailor's problems. The man deserved to have his luck back again. After all, he had been kind. He had even said Elvis could stay at his house if he didn't mind soggy carpets. Which Elvis did. They had parted the best of friends.

It had made Elvis feel very bad indeed to see the havoc he had caused Mr. Rollo. It was clear the tailor had intended to thank him, unlike Sir Walter Cross, who never once had said "How are you?" let alone "Thank you."

"It was all his fault," said Elvis out loud. "But I never meant him to be murdered."

He was standing at the time in Podgy Bottom High Street. Already he'd had some funny looks from passersby. One woman with a buggy the size of a tank had asked him if he was starring in the local pantomime.

"No," said Elvis, appalled. "I am not."

"No need to be so rude," said the woman, and she walked away.

"Rude? Me? Rude?" said Elvis under his breath. "It's human beings like Sir Walter Cross and Pan Smith who have no manners. No manners at all."

It was so unfair. He had come to visit the human world out of the goodness of his heart, to make wishes come true. The only trouble was that human beings were never happy with one wish. They always wanted more—and then some. Elvis, being a well-brought-up elf, didn't like to refuse. And he enjoyed seeing the amazed looks on their faces when the impossible came true. All he wanted in return was one simple thank-you. Was it so very much to ask?

"I shouldn't have gone to Toff the Terrible," said Elvis to himself. "And I wouldn't have, if it hadn't been for the umbrella. I shouldn't have told Toff about all the other wishes I granted, either. Oh dear, what a mess." He brightened a little. "I will make everything better as far as I can."

Next on the list of things to be put right was Pan Smith.

Elvis tried to think about all she had wished for, but it was such a long list that it was impossible to remember. Hair? That was it. Hair. Elvis couldn't recall whether she had wanted blond, red, black, pink, or blue hair. He saw it as being bright pink. Or was that another lady? Elvis had to admit to being in a muddle. He had handed out so many wishes that it had all become a rather big blur. He was certain that Pan had wished to have a different figure, but was it thin, fat, or chubby? Again he was confused.

It was then that he saw a newsstand, and as it

had started to snow, he went inside to warm up and study the women's magazines.

He could only reach the bottom two shelves. First of all, he took down a magazine with pretty ladies on the front cover and flicked through the pictures. There was one that took his fancy. It was of a rather curvy lady,

 and next to her was a photo of a very trim lady. The captions read "Before" and "After."

Before what and after what? Elvis wasn't sure, but there was no doubt in his mind that the before lady looked far prettier than the after lady. Who wanted to cuddle up to a bag of bones? So now he knew exactly what Pan Smith needed—long, thick, pink hair and a body as round as an apple.

Next was to put the house back in order. This part would be simple. He found a wedding magazine and again flicked through the pictures. There were so many dull, white wedding dresses. No color, thought Elvis.

Who would want to be married without an

explosion of color? He found a wedding dress in the magazine he thought would suit the new Pan Smith if he added his own touches. He had always seen himself as an artist, and interior design was just up his street, with bells on. He had a wonderful plan for the dining room and the tent. With these happy thoughts in his mind, he made his way to Mountview Drive. If he could put two rights together, it might make up for the one terrible wrong.

It was much later that day that his eye was caught by the headline of the evening paper.

TAILOR ARRESTED
WITH FIVE BAGS OF GOLD

"Oh no!" said Elvis. "I must do something—but what?"

Chapter Seventeen

In the whirlwind of kidnapping the magic lamp, Toff the Terrible had accidentally taken the dog as well.

He had never been that keen on dogs. This one barked loudly and, worse still, nipped the ankle of any passing goblin. If the magic lamp hadn't been so crucial to his plan, he would have kicked it out by now. How anyone put up with the thing, Toff had no idea. It bossed everyone about—and the dog snapped at any goblins who didn't do what the lamp ordered.

The lamp had the goblins cleaning up. So far, the carpets had been vacuumed—Toff hadn't known they even owned a vacuum—the table and floor had been scrubbed, the beds changed, the sheets washed, and the clothes neatly folded away. As for the kitchen, it looked completely different. They did have a sink after all and, even more surprisingly, an oven and fridge.

"We are warriors!" said Toff the Terrible, and beat his chest to prove it.

But all the magic lamp said was "I hope your room's tidy. There will be no supper for goblins with untidy rooms."

"Now, look here, shiny belly, I am Toff the Terrible. Do you know what I do to lamps like you? Scrap metal!"

The magic lamp chuckled.

And this was the part Toff the Terrible couldn't understand. Whether they liked it or not, the goblins did whatever the magic lamp told them to.

At breakfast time that evening, they all sat down to eat. The table was laid with a checked tablecloth and a posy of flowers. All the goblins had brushed their hair and beards. It was enough to make Toff the Terrible feel like giving up, especially when one of his gang asked him politely if he wouldn't mind please passing the pepper.

This had to stop. Had they forgotten why they had kidnapped the lamp in the first place? He would put an end to all this namby-pamby preschool activity. As for the dog, it was dead meat.

That night, when the lamp and Doughnut had gone to bed, Toff the Terrible locked them in their room and called an emergency meeting.

"What are you waiting for? Make that piece of scrap metal open its lid. Take it down to the dungeon and see if it comes to its senses."

None of his gang of goblins seemed that keen on the plan anymore.

"What's wrong with you all?" he asked.

"The lamp said it would make all our beards fall out if we hurt it," said one goblin.

"It can't," said Toff, none too certain if that was correct or not.

"Yes, it can," said all the goblins together.

"No, it can't. We have until bedtime tomorrow morning to make that lamp open its lid."

In the guest room with Doughnut, the magic lamp was trying to think up a plan for their escape. It didn't know why they had been kidnapped, but it was certain that it had nothing to do with housekeeping. Now, in the quiet of the night, everything felt a lot more scary. Outside an owl hooted.

"They could kill us while we sleep," said the magic lamp. "Who would ever know?"

Doughnut started barking the second he heard the sound of goblins outside the guest room door. As quickly as they could, they scrambled under the bed from where they could see the hairy toes of the goblins as they stormed into the room, each holding a baseball bat.

"No, no, don't," squeaked the lamp, as it was pulled from its hiding place by two goblins. "You're making a terrible mistake!"

Doughnut followed them, growling and nipping the goblins' ankles.

In the dungeon, Toff the Terrible stood waiting.

"What are you going to do to me?" said the lamp, its little knees knocking together.

A gruesome smile spread across Toff the Terrible's face.

"We can do this the friendly way or the unfriendly way."

"What's the friendly way?" asked the magic lamp.

"You just open that lid of yours."

"No, never!" said the lamp bravely. "I made that mistake once before. Never again, I tell you. Never again!"

"Listen here, you tin-pot piece of junk, if you don't open that lid, it's the Vaseline treatment for you. Failing that, WD-40. And if that doesn't work, then it will come down to the good old-fashioned twist. It always worked on the lids of my mum's gooseberry jam."

"Oh, woe is me," cried the magic lamp.

The Band of Baddies giggled, pleased to find their beards hadn't fallen out. As they turned the key in the lock, the lamp could be heard wailing.

"Don't leave me here all alone! Oh, sweet mistress, where are you? Help me, someone, help me."

Doughnut howled in reply.

"What do we do with the dog, boss?" asked one of the Band of Baddies.

"Tie him up," ordered Toff. "We'll deal with him later."

Doughnut had other plans. No goblin was going to tie him up. He charged past the Band of Baddies, tripping up two of them and nipping a third.

"Catch that dog, you fools," roared Toff the Terrible.

Ears flapping, Doughnut ran at tremendous speed up the stone spiral staircase and along a winding passageway to the Great Hall, where more goblins were waiting to pounce on him.

But Doughnut was too fast for the stout goblins. He dived through their legs and out into the snow. All that was on Doughnut's mind was to find his way back to Wings & Co. He had only gone a few yards when he realized his troubles were just beginning. The snow was as deep as he was tall.

Chapter Eighteen

ou are a cat," said Sergeant Litton of the Podgy Bottom Police. Fidget had asked him if the tailor would soon be released. "I can't go talking to cats."

"I have a medical condition," said Fidget. "Would you please tell me if Mr. Rollo has been charged?"

"Not precisely," replied the sergeant. "We believe he has robbed a bank."

"Which bank, precisely, did he rob?" asked Fidget.

"That's the thing," said Sergeant Litton. "We are not precisely sure which bank it is. But it has to be a bank."

"Why?" asked Emily, who had gone to the police station with Fidget to see if she could be of help.

"Because," said Sergeant Litton, a little puffed up with his own importance, "no one has five sacks of gold coins fall out of the sky and land at his feet."

"Maybe he won the lottery," suggested Emily helpfully.

Sergeant Litton huffed.

"In gold coins? I don't think so," he said.

After a wait of half an hour or so, the bedraggled tailor was brought up from the cells.

"Oh, Mr. Fidget," said Mr. Rollo. "Well, here you are. What a pleasant sight. So comforting to see such a well-made cat costume."

"Come along," said Fidget kindly, putting a paw on the tailor's shoulder.

"What a day. Well, one of the worst, that's all, one of the worst. Am I free to go?" the tailor asked Sergeant Litton.

Emily could tell that Sergeant Litton much preferred locking people up to letting them out.

"No charges will be pressed at the present time," he said.

"What about the five sacks of gold coins?" asked Emily. "What will happen to them?"

"They will stay with us until the investigation has been completed," said the sergeant.

"Well, if Rosalind knew about this, I hate to think what she'd say," said Mr. Rollo. "And her mother— well, that would be the end of it all, and no mistake."

Fidget and Emily, seeing how upset the tailor was, thought it best to take him back to Wings & Co.

Buster had stayed in the shop. He was busy studying back copies of *Fairy World International*, looking for any similar mischief.

He hoped to find a report of someone in the fairy world who had been overgenerous in granting wishes. Instead, Buster had come across an ad for information leading to the whereabouts of Elvis the Elf. The ad had been put in by the missing elf's parents. They described him as a happy, generous elf who loved his mum and dad. He had gone out one day with his new umbrella

and had never come home. His disappearance was a mystery. Buster found three more such notices, and there was even a picture of Elvis as a young lad. He beamed at the camera through a fistful of freckles.

Buster knew elves were, on the whole, home-loving creatures, neat and tidy. They lived in forests and found towns confusing, so why, he wondered, had this elf not returned to his family? He whirled around in the office chair while he pondered the problem. Maybe the clue to the elf's disappearance lay in the umbrella. An elf umbrella was a very powerful piece of equipment and had all sorts of magic properties.

If he had lost it, he would be stuck, unable to return home. But no elf, as far as Buster knew, ever willingly gave up an umbrella to anyone, and the idea that he would have lost it was just plain daft. Without their umbrellas, elves couldn't fly. It was then that it struck him. If an elf's umbrella fell into the wrong hands, its magic could be used to . . .

"Buddleia," said Buster out loud. "And buddleia again. The sooner that umbrella's found, the better."

He whizzed faster and faster in the swivel chair, his thoughts a merry-go-round of ideas. Then he saw on the pavement outside the blurry figures of Fidget, Emily, and someone who he thought must be Mr. Rollo. Buster sprang up and opened the shop door.

"Welcome," he said, greeting the tailor. "I am Buster Ignatius Spicer. Here to help you."

"That is most kind," said Mr. Rollo. "Most kind, well, indeed."

They took the poor man upstairs and sat him down near the fire to get warm. Fidget went to make tea.

Mr. Rollo cheered up at the sight of the green and red cupcakes.

"Tell me what happened," said Buster, when Mr. Rollo looked more himself.

The tailor told them.

"One minute I was walking along, minding my own ruin, and the next minute, in my hands were two heavy bags. Well, I nearly fell over, for at my feet were three more bags. They all contained gold coins. I didn't know what to do. They each had a label on which my name was written. Well, I hailed a taxi, and to my surprise, the taxi driver, well, he took me to the police station. The driver said he was certain I was a burglar. Me. Well. Well, I never."

"What happened before the gold coins fell from the sky?" asked Emily, handing the tailor a cupcake.

Mr. Rollo told them about Mr. Elvis Elf and about the vest and the reason he had made it for him in the first place.

"Good," said Buster. "Very good."

"Well, not really," said Mr. Rollo.

Buster showed him the picture he had found of the elf.

"Why," cried Mr. Rollo, "that is Mr. Elvis Elf."

Emily and Fidget leaned over to look.

"It's hard to imagine," said Emily, "that this sweet-looking elf could be responsible for the murder of Sir Walter Cross."

"Murder?" said the tailor. "Well, that's impossible. He's such a well-brought-up young man."

"I think you might be right," said Fidget.

"Then who did bump him off?" asked Emily.

"That," said Buster, "is what we are here to find out."

Chapter Nineteen

Pan Smith felt as if she had woken from a bad dream. What had she been thinking of when she had agreed to marry Kyle Pots? And more to the point, how could she ever have been so stupid as to lose Derek, the best man in the world? Pan looked in the mirror as she put on her lipstick. She was about to say, "I wish . . ." when she stopped herself. She knew this much: If she wanted Derek, she would have to win him back herself. No amount of wishing would be able to do it.

Her mother, Pauline, was in the kitchen making another trifle in the hope that the wedding might be on again.

"Where are you going?" she called.

"To see Derek, Mum," said Pan. "I need to talk to him."

"But what about Kyle Pots?" asked her mother.

"He never loved me, not like Derek did," said Pan. "I'm borrowing your coat—the one with the hood—okay?"

She put on her mum's coat and opened the front door.

"Wait," said her mother. "Pan, Kyle is rich and a member of the golf club."

"Derek is rich in love, Mum," said Pan. And with that, she left.

Life, thought Pauline Smith, could not get any worse.

By the time Elvis made his next big mistake, it was starting to snow once more. He had arrived at Twenty-two Mountview Drive and hidden in the garden behind a myrtle bush. Elvis wasn't entirely sure, but he thought it was Mrs. Smith who had driven off in the car. Mr. Smith would be at work. He waited a little longer, then tiptoed to the window and, standing on a flowerpot, peeked into the living room. The falling snow and the net curtains made it hard to see in, but he could just make out the blurred shape of a lady fast asleep in an armchair. That must be Pan Smith, thought Elvis, who by now was very cold indeed. What with all the waiting around, his fingers were numb and so were his toes. It was hard to think when you were in a freezer. The sooner he cast his spell, the better.

He gave the sleeping lady the hair and figure she had always wanted—or so he thought—then crept around to the dining room and peered through the French windows. He would have it all in order in no time. He cast another of his spells, leaving the box containing the wedding dress on the table, all tied up with a big bow. He turned his attention successfully to the tent and sighed with relief. Once he had sorted out Mr. Rollo, his heart would be lighter, knowing that there had been a happy ending for all. All except Sir Walter Cross, of course, but Elvis tried not to think about him.

He was just about to leave when two things happened at roughly the same time. Mr. Smith, who had not gone to work, went into the living room with a tea tray just as the car pulled up and Pan and Derek got out.

"Pauline!" came a cry from the lounge. "Pauline!"

Elvis inched along the wall, back to the living room window.

Mr. Smith had switched on a lamp, and Elvis could see a teapot and cups lying broken on the floor. Pauline Smith was staring at herself in the mirror over the fireplace. Pan and Derek rushed in.

"Mum!" shrieked Pan. "Oh, Mum, what's happened?"

"Well, blow me down," said Harry Smith. "You look . . ."

"Yes?" said his wife, turning to him. "Terrible?" she suggested.

"No," said Harry. "You look . . . magical."

Elvis couldn't hear what they'd said to each other; all he knew was that once again he had made a right pickle of the whole business. It was a mess, and no mistake.

Miserable, Elvis the Elf wandered into the woods at the end of Mountview Drive. Maybe he would never get his umbrella back, never be able to go home, never see his mum and dad again.

The snow lay thick on the ground. Elvis had been walking for some time, and the light was beginning to fade when he heard a muffled growl and then a muffled yap. *Doughnut*, he thought. *It's Doughnut. I would know that yap anywhere. But where is he?* All Elvis could see was glittering snow. He followed the sound to what looked like a small snowdrift beneath a tree. Elvis crouched, scraped away the snow, and there he found the little dog. He carefully lifted Doughnut up and brushed the ice from his fish knit coat.

Once out of the woods, Elvis put Doughnut down on the pavement, uncertain where to go. He decided that the best plan was to follow the dog. After all, he seemed to know his way home, which was more than Elvis did.

Chapter Twenty

By the time Doughnut and Elvis reached Wings & Co., the moon hung above the shop like a huge silver balloon tied by a silken thread to one of the shop's crooked chimney pots.

The moonlight spilled down the alleyway toward them.

Emily was locking up when she spotted the woebegone pair. She rushed outside to greet them.

"Thank goodness you're safe," she said to Doughnut, picking him up. "I've been so worried. Where's the lamp?" She turned to Elvis. "And you—are you okay?"

Elvis shyly took off his bright green hat and bowed. "I am rather lost," he said.

"Come into the warm," said Emily, and Elvis followed her into the shop and up the stairs.

Buster was sprawled on the sofa, engrossed in *Fairy World International*, while Fidget sat in the armchair, knitting fishes. The tailor had gone to bed with a hot water bottle and a cup of cocoa. He was exhausted by all that had happened to him and was very grateful to have such a comfortable place to sleep.

Emily opened the living room door, and Doughnut rushed in and leapt upon Fidget, frantically licking his face.

"I think he missed you," said Buster.

"Seems he is trying to say something," said Fidget.

"It's such a pity none of us speak Dog," said Emily.

Meanwhile, Elvis, hat in hand, was hiding in the

shadows on the landing. Emily gently pulled him into the room.

"Elvis Elf," said Buster.

"You know my name?" said Elvis, impressed.

"Yes," said Buster. "Of course I do. You are the prime suspect in the murder of Sir Walter Cross."

"No!" said Elvis. "No, no, I didn't . . . oh, what a mess. It was Toff the Terrible, I only—"

"Toff the Terrible?" interrupted Buster, sitting up.

"Yes," said Elvis.

"Are you absolutely sure?" asked Buster.

"Quite sure," said Elvis. "He lives beneath the big oak tree in the woods. He's a goblin."

"I know," said Buster, and muttered something under his breath. "How in all the meddling muddles did you become involved with that Band of Baddies? I bet you all the toffee in the trees that it's Toff the Terrible who kidnapped the magic lamp."

"I had nothing to do with that," said Elvis. "Oh dear, oh dear."

He twisted the brim of his hat and looked more

and more wretched. Emily could see he was about to burst into tears.

"Have you eaten?" she asked him.

"No," said Elvis. "Not for ages."

"Why don't you sit down by the fire," she said kindly, "and we will make tea."

"Fishcakes?" said Fidget.

Elvis nodded.

"Spot on," said Fidget as he left the room.

"Oh, what a mess," said Elvis. "I never murdered anyone, never. I couldn't, I have a sensitive throat."

"What's that got to do with it?" asked Buster.

"Quiet, Buster," said Emily. "Mr. Elf—Elvis—why don't you start at the beginning?"

"All right," said Elvis. "The once-upon-a-time beginning or my beginning?"

"Yours," said Buster.

Elvis took a deep breath.

"Mum and Dad had just given me my first umbrella," said the elf. "It was supercharged, and they thought it might be a bit advanced for me. I was so

excited. I had heard about humans and how they liked to wish for things. In fact, Mum thought that humans did nothing but wish. I wanted to see for myself, just for a morning, and as I had my umbrella, I could. From the air, I saw this lovely garden with a duck pond and decided that was the place to land. I was just noticing that the grass was green, the sky was blue, and so far all was the same as where we lived, when someone grabbed me. He demanded to know what I was doing on his private property. I said I was an elf and had come to see the human world and grant a few wishes. Then he asked why I had an umbrella on such a hot day."

The mention of the umbrella caused a tear to roll down Elvis's cheek. He was about to go on with his tale when Fidget arrived with a plate piled high with fishcakes and french fries. Emily went to help with the tea.

They sat by the fire, eating and staring at the logs as they hissed and crackled.

"Better?" asked Emily, after Elvis had wiped his mouth and neatly put his knife and fork together.

"Much, thank you."

"Good," said Buster. "The umbrella?"

"Yes. I explained to the man—Sir Walter Cross—that was how I'd arrived there. He asked me what would happen if I didn't have my umbrella, and like the biggest chump ever, I told him."

"He took the umbrella away, didn't he?" said Buster.

"Yes," sobbed Elvis. "And without it, I couldn't go home to Mum and Dad. He promised he would give it back if I granted his wish, which was to know the name of the winner of a horse race. I kept my word, but he kept my umbrella."

"That was horrid of him," said Emily.

"Yes," said Elvis, blowing his nose on a purple-spotted handkerchief. "Every day he would wave my umbrella in front of me, then, when I gave him another winner, put it back in his coat pocket. I didn't know what to do. Then I met Toff the Terrible, and he said he would help me."

"And did he help you?" asked Emily.

"No, he just made everything worse. Worse than worse. He did dreadful things, and now he has my umbrella."

Chapter Twenty-one

The following morning, Emily woke to find her bedroom door had shrunk to dollhouse size. She lay flat on her tummy and opened the door with her finger. Doughnut ran past, then back again.

"Hello," she called.

Doughnut stopped and lay down, his head to one side, puzzled that he couldn't go into the room for a cuddle.

Then he ran away.

Emily was alarmed. Something was terribly wrong. But there was little she could do about it other than wait patiently until the old shop sorted itself out, which Emily knew would happen sooner or later. The sooner the

better, she thought, and went back to bed and snuggled under the covers. It was deliciously warm. She lay staring at the ceiling. She was certain Buster knew more than he was letting on—he seemed convinced that the magic lamp had been kidnapped by goblins. Perhaps he was working on a hunch like all detectives do. But what was it? And why was he keeping it to himself? Bored with bed and unanswerable questions, Emily decided she had better dress and be ready for action.

It was well past lunchtime when the door decided to grow back to its old size again. She opened it, and there stood Fidget holding a plate of buttered toast and a mug of tea for her.

"What's going on?" asked Emily. She was now rather hungry, and buttered toast seemed just the ticket.

"A moldy kipper of a mess, that's for sure," said Fidget. "Elvis Elf was kidnapped last night."

Emily felt her knees go weak. It was a disaster.

"Who . . . why . . . when? I mean, that shouldn't be possible."

"Spot on the fishcake, my little ducks. It seems the shop went into lockdown. It must have become confused, what with the tailor and Elvis Elf sleeping here. It looks like it let in Toff the Terrible by mistake."

"Oh, Fidget, that's dreadful," said Emily. "You don't think that Elvis has gone . . ." She stopped. It was too awful a thought. ". . . The same way as Sir Walter Cross?"

"I hope not," said Fidget. "But there are drops of blood in the shop."

Emily gasped. "What are we going to do?"

"Search my catnip, I don't know," said Fidget.

"Where's Mr. Rollo?" said Emily, as she put on her boots.

"That's the one good thing. He's still fast asleep, snoring like a trouper. The longer he stays that way, the better. His door is only halibut high at the moment, and if he were to wake, it would take some explaining."

"Quite. Where's Buster?" asked Emily.

"Upstairs in the library."

"Library?" said Emily. "I didn't know we had one."

"To tell you the truth," said Fidget, "I, too, had forgotten about it. It's up in the attic. Or it was half an hour ago."

Sure enough, there it was. The whole of the attic was lined with books. Some were flying through the air like brightly colored birds, flapping their pages, while others rested in piles on a long table. Buster was sitting at a desk with a huge book before him. He didn't even look up when Emily came in.

"Are you ready?" he asked her.

"Yes," said Emily, uncertain what exactly she should be ready for.

"We are going to rescue Elvis and bring back the lamp," said Buster, still engrossed in his book.

Fidget came puffing up the stairs.

"Buddleia," he said under his breath. "Too many stairs. I think they keep multiplying on purpose." In his paws he held a sword.

"This is for you, Buster. A treasure from Miss String's painted oak chest."

"Wow," said Emily. "Do you really think Buster will need it?"

"Yes, my little ducks," said Fidget. "Toff the Terrible is a very dangerous goblin."

Buster took the sword from its scabbard. It was as light as a magic wand.

"Anything special about it?" Buster asked hopefully.

"Yes," said Fidget. "But the trouble is, my dear old shrimp, I can't remember what."

"Try," said Buster. "A clue would help. Like, who did it belong to?"

"A knight who wore green socks," replied Fidget.

"That's all? Green socks?" said Buster.

"Yep. There was also something about justice and honor."

"Nothing more?"

"Nope," said Fidget. "That's all that has stayed glued to the fishing hooks of my memory."

"I've been thinking," said Emily. "Why would a goblin want the magic lamp in the first place? I mean, it's useless—it doesn't have a genie or anything like that."

"Of course!" said Buster, furiously flicking the pages of the book. "How could I have been so stupid? That's it."

"That's what, my old haddock?" asked Fidget.

Buster slammed the book shut. Dust rose from the pages. He put the sword back in its scabbard and strapped it around him.

"I'll explain later. Come on, Emily, we have an elf and a magic lamp to rescue before it's too late."

Chapter Twenty-two

By the time the shop had returned to normal, it was teatime, and Mr. Rollo had woken up feeling as fresh as a daisy. The sun was setting on the thick snow, and he felt better than he had done for weeks. Fortunately he knew nothing about the drama that had gone on all around him.

He told Fidget he was going to see Rosalind and ask her to come home—soggy carpets or no soggy carpets.

"An excellent idea," said Fidget, much relieved. This was not a good day to be at Wings & Co.

As the tailor left, Lettice Lovage arrived. Unlike Mr. Rollo, she was not in the best of moods.

"I thought you were supposed to be detectives. Why

haven't you found that elf yet?" she said to Fidget. "Pan's told me all about that wicked little creature, and I want a word with him."

"Now wait a mo, my old mackerel," said Fidget. "Elvis was here, but last night he was kidnapped—by Toff the Terrible, we believe."

"You mean you caught that elf, and now he's gone?"

"Yes," said Fidget. "But—"

"Do you know what mischief he's made at Mountview Drive?"

"No," said Fidget. "But—"

"He only gave my friend Pauline Smith bright pink hair and the body shape of an apple. Not to mention what he did to the dining room, the tent, and the wedding dress. I'll tell you this, deary—"

"Listen to me, my old mackerel," said Fidget. "Buster and Emily have gone to rescue Elvis the Elf."

"Rescue?" said Lettice. "What's going on?"

"Elvis came here for help," said Fidget. "And last night he was kidnapped by Toff the Terrible, who, by the way, also has the magic lamp."

"Why didn't you say so straightaway?" said Lettice.

"I did," said Fidget.

"You mean that no-good, murderous goblin has the elf?"

"Spot on the fishcake," said Fidget.

"I don't mind what happens to that lamp, deary, but I want first pop at Elvis the Elf."

It was then that Doughnut came bouncing into the shop and started to yap.

Lettice yapped back. This went on for quite some time until at last Doughnut had said his piece.

Lettice picked up the little dog and sat down in a chair with him on her lap.

"Toff the Terrible has the lamp locked in a dungeon, threatening to do I don't know what to it if it won't open its lid. This is much more serious than I first thought, deary."

"What else did Doughnut say, old trout?" asked Fidget.

"That his master was a downright bully."

Doughnut's complaints were many. Lack of proper walks, shouting, forgetting to feed him, and once, leaving him locked out all night to howl at that huge silver ball

in the sky. If things hadn't looked that jolly from a miniature dachshund's point of view, then they looked downright terrible for Elvis the Elf. The master had caught him one day near the duck pond and taken away his cloth stick.

"His umbrella, perhaps?" said Fidget.

"Yes, that's right, deary," said Lettice.

Elvis had asked for it back, it being a very important kind of stick, but the cloth stick was never returned. Then one day, Doughnut and his master were down by the duck pond when a fiery goblin turned up. His master had barked at the goblin and barked again. He wouldn't give the cloth stick to the goblin either. The goblin pulled one way and his master the other. That's when both dog and master shot up into the air. Doughnut landed safely; his master didn't.

"Where was Elvis all this time?" asked Fidget.

"Tied to the willow tree," said Lettice, putting Doughnut back on the floor.

Lettice Lovage rummaged in her handbag for her lipstick and blush. She touched up her face in a mirror before snapping shut her handbag and standing up.

"I'm off," she said.

"Where to?" asked Fidget.

"Where do you think, deary?" she said. "I can't leave my nephew and Emily Vole to fight Toff the Terrible on their own. This is one murderous goblin we are dealing with. He must be stopped at all costs. And I still want a word with that elf."

Chapter Twenty-three

It was growing dark by the time Buster and Emily arrived at the goblin den. They had made a plan to outwit Toff the Terrible without using magic as, sad to say, neither of them had been able to work out the riddle of the sword.

"Maybe there's no riddle to work out. Maybe we only think it's magical because it came from Miss String's magical chest," said Emily.

The wooden door creaked open, sounding louder than a hundred rusty trumpets.

"That should bring the goblins running," said Buster.

"I'll find somewhere to hide," whispered Emily.

No goblins came.

Buster held his sword out before him and stepped into the middle of the Great Hall as Emily quickly slid behind a smelly sheepskin that was hanging on the wall.

Still no goblins came.

"Come out, come out, wherever you are," shouted Buster.

But no goblins came out from wherever they were.

In the gloom it was hard to see anything, the hall being only half lit by a hideous chandelier made from deer horns. Hanging from one of the antlers was Elvis's green hat.

Under the chandelier was a long wooden table piled high with dirty plates, goblets, twisted-up sweet wrappers, and half-eaten packets of cereal. The benches on both sides of the table had been knocked over. Buster was about to go farther into the den when the light went on and he found that he was surrounded on all sides by goblins.

"Got you!" shouted Toff the Terrible, and raised his dagger. "This time, you are dead fairy meat!" he roared.

"This time"? Emily thought. *What does he mean by "this time"?* The sheepskin made her want to sneeze. She

pinched her nose and waited for an opportunity to make her move.

In a tight situation, Buster was good at thinking on his feet—and this was one of the tightest situations he had been in for ages.

"If you're determined to kill me," he said, "couldn't you at least do it fairly and squarely with a good, swashbuckling fight?"

"I could just kill you with this dagger," said Toff the Terrible.

Which was true.

"But where's the fun in that?" said Buster.

"Mmm, you have a point," said Toff. "I do like a good fight to the death, especially if it's toe-curlingly grim." He turned to one of the Baddies. "Bring me my sword," he ordered.

"No magic tricks, mind you," said Buster, seeing the size of Toff's sword. "Just a good old-fashioned fight."

"Agreed," said Toff the Terrible.

"Also," added Buster, "if I win, I want Elvis the Elf and the lamp back."

Toff the Terrible started to laugh.

"If you win? Now, that's funny."

Toff the Terrible had no style when it came to sword fighting. He was all roars and grunts. His main line of attack was to lift his weapon high over his head and try to bring it down on top of Buster, just as you would a fly swatter on a fly. Fortunately, Buster was faster and nimbler.

It didn't take him long to wrong-foot Toff the Terrible, who slipped on a half-eaten chocolate. Buster felt he had the situation under control.

All the goblins were gathered around the fight, egging on their boss. Emily knew this was her best chance to slip away. She ran silently down the passage until she came to a stone spiral staircase.

The thing about goblins is they don't play fair. The second it looked as if Buster was winning, Toff the Terrible's sword turned into a serpent with a two-pronged tongue. It appeared determined to gobble Buster up.

"You cheat!" shouted Buster, as the snake lashed out at him.

"Hee hee hee," laughed Toff the Terrible. "This will be the end of you!"

Buster fought off the creature, managing to land a fatal blow to its head, but Toff's sword changed again, this time into the tail of a scaly dragon. It swished back and forth with alarming force.

"Pathetic," said Buster. "Is that the best you can do?"

"No," said Toff the Terrible, and the dragon's tail bashed Buster's sword out of his hand. Toff picked it up. "Just an ordinary sword," he said. "With no magic."

Then something extraordinary happened, something Buster hadn't been expecting. The sword turned to ice in Toff the Terrible's hand, and he began to freeze. Even his beard turned frosty. Toff the Terrible instantly threw the sword on the ground and stood well back. The goblin leader looked terrified.

"Where did you get this?" he asked.

"It once belonged to a knight who wore green socks," said Buster.

"A knight who wore green—"

He was interrupted by a voice, a voice that both Toff the Terrible and Buster knew and feared.

"Cooeee—are you there, deary?"

Chapter Twenty-four

Lettice Lovage stood at the doorway of the Great Hall, wrapped in a puffer coat and swinging her handbag.

"All this trudging through the snow," she complained, as she took off her coat. "I don't know why goblins have to live in dens. It's beyond me. No modern conveniences—so yesterday."

Toff the Terrible stared at her, openmouthed. She delved into her handbag for her magic wand.

"And not even a hook to hang my coat on."

She flicked her wand, and instantly her coat was hanging on an invisible coat hanger. She flicked her wand again, and there she was, dressed in a glimmering golden gown, a crown on her head, her wings iridescent. Slowly at first, she grew taller and taller—so tall that her head touched the beams of the Great Hall.

Toff the Terrible gulped, for Lettice Lovage wasn't your average common or garden fairy. No, she was a fairy godmother, and you don't become a fairy godmother without possessing considerable powers. Golden coaches, glass slippers, and Prince Charmings are all very well, but they are the pretty part of the job. When faced with a goblin den, pretty is forgotten, along with the glass slipper.

Lettice waved her wand, and all the goblins were pinned to the back wall of the Great Hall, their knobbly knees shaking.

"Where is Emily Vole?" demanded Lettice.

"She went to find Elvis the Elf and the magic lamp," said Buster.

Lettice waved her wand again, and Emily appeared, cradling the magic lamp, its arms and legs all floppy. The elf stood beside her, his finger bandaged and his precious umbrella clutched in his other hand.

Emily, speechless, stared up at the amazing apparition that was Lettice Lovage.

"What happened?" said Buster.

"I'm not sure," said Emily. "I found the dungeon, looked through the bars, and there they were. The lamp said, 'Oh, sweet mistress,' and then just keeled over."

"Oh, what a mess," said Elvis. "Now I've murdered the lamp as well."

"No, you haven't," said Buster. "It's just fainted."

The lamp began to come to.

"Tell me, sweet mistress, I am safe," it said, lifting a hand to its lid. Glancing up, it saw Lettice Lovage towering over them and passed out again.

"What have you to say for yourself, Elvis Elf?" asked Lettice.

"I'm very sorry. I am terribly sorry," he said. "I did wrong."

"Yes," agreed Lettice. "You, deary, are a stupid, half-baked, foolish numbskull of an elf."

"Hold on, Auntie," said Buster. "That's a bit steep."

"However you put it, there is still an elf at the bottom of this case," said Lettice.

"Yes, but . . ." Buster didn't finish what he was saying.

"How many wishes did you hand out?" Lettice asked the elf.

"I can't remember—it's all such a blur," said Elvis. "Oh, what a mess."

"Hee hee," laughed Toff the Terrible, who enjoyed seeing other people being told off.

"Quiet, you snot-filled goblin!" Lettice seemed to grow even bigger.

"Toff the Terrible, you are charged with the murder of Sir Walter Cross, ruining Mr. Rollo's business, and making one humongous mess of Pan Smith's wedding arrangements."

"May I interrupt you, Aunt Lettice?" said Buster.

"Yes, deary, go ahead."

"Toff the Terrible, you also stole the magic lamp with the intention of installing a genie."

"I didn't. I wouldn't. I couldn't get its lid off."

"I know what you were up to," said Buster. "I know

the spell. By putting Elvis's supercharged umbrella inside the magic lamp, you hoped to conjure up a genie who would make you all-powerful."

"None of it is my fault. Look, if anyone should be charged with these crimes, it's—"

"Silence!" roared Lettice, and her voice rumbled so loudly around the Great Hall that a huge piece of plaster fell from the ceiling and landed at Toff the Terrible's hairy feet.

Lettice turned to her nephew. "Be a love—put your sword on Toff's shoulder."

"No, no," said Toff. "Please, pretty please . . . spare me. Anything but that!"

"Anything but what?" asked Buster.

"He went blue when he touched it, didn't he, deary? Started to freeze," said Lettice.

"Yes," said Buster.

"The first stage, deary, of being turned to stone," said his aunt.

"Stone?" repeated Buster.

"Fidget gave you the Sword of Justice," said Lettice. "Didn't he tell you?"

"No," said Buster, looking at it, impressed. "Just something about green socks."

"Yes, deary, and the Sword of Justice has found Toff the Terrible guilty as charged and will turn him into stone for a hundred years. Just rest it on the goblin's shoulder, and we are done and dusted."

"What about the Band of Baddies?" asked Buster.

"Stone for the lot of them, I say," said Lettice. "I'll sell them to a garden center."

The goblins all began to wail.

"Spare us, please, please!"

"Quiet," said Lettice. "Quiet! There is an *or*."

"An *or*?" whimpered Toff the Terrible, nibbling the end of his beard. "What kind of *or*?"

Lettice sighed and returned to her normal size.

"Or," she said, "you work in the community."

"You what?" said Toff.

"It's simple, deary. It means that I put a spell on these woods so that you can't leave. Instead you will have to work."

"Work!" moaned Toff the Terrible. "Me, work? Work at what?"

"You and the Band of Baddies will look after the woods, pick up rubbish, and clear away dog poo. And be kind to children, for they will be able to see you."

"No, no," wailed Toff the Terrible. "Isn't there another *or* to be had?"

"No. The choice is yours. Garden gnomes or pooper scoopers."

Toff the Terrible and the Band of Baddies huddled together in a corner to discuss their options.

"Well done, Auntie," said Buster.

Lettice looked at him. "You didn't do so badly yourself," she said. "Come here and give me a kiss."

And it was then, just as his aunt was about to plant a kiss on his cheek, that to everyone's surprise, Buster vanished into thin air.

"A pooper scooper it is," said a mournful Toff the Terrible.

Chapter Twenty-five

$\mathcal{F}$idget was minding the shop when he noticed one of the keys rushing to and fro. It jumped up and down near the curious cabinets as if it was trying to reach the top drawer. Gingerly, Fidget went to see if he could help. The key seemed relieved to see him. It climbed onto his paw and waited to be lifted up. Only when it was near the drawer it wanted did it jump into a keyhole, head first, its little legs sticking out. Then with a huge sigh, it turned itself in the lock.

The next thing happened so suddenly that it was a bit of a blur. Fidget saw an incredibly bright light spring from the drawer itself—so bright, in fact, that it half blinded him. When he could see straight again, there was Buster. He had appeared from nowhere, surrounded by a silver haze. It took quite a few moments to work out that what he was seeing was Buster Ignatius Spicer with wings.

"You've got them back, my dear old shrimp!" shouted Fidget.

At that moment, they were interrupted by the sudden arrival of Lettice, Elvis, and Emily, who was carrying the magic lamp. They skidded through the door, trailing stardust behind them.

As Lettice came to a stop, she saw Buster.

"I thought so, deary," she said. "I told Emily not to worry. I'm so glad you have your wings back at last."

"I do," said Buster, laughing. "I do. I'm now going to be all grown up, just like James Cardwell. You wait and see. In a moment, it will happen."

They waited. The silver light began to vanish from around Buster, and when the room came back into focus, he found that he was just the same as before. He hadn't grown up, not by one year, not by one minute.

"Oh," said Buster, seeing his reflection in the glass. "I'm still eleven."

"I think, my old mackerels," said Fidget, taking the lamp from Emily and guiding Lettice and Elvis to the stairs, "we deserve a special celebration tea."

"There's no place like home," the lamp called out feebly.

Emily thought that perhaps she should wait for Buster, so she sat on the counter, dangling her legs and staring out of the shop window. Buster had his back to her. It gave Emily a chance to study his wings. They were small and quite beautiful, with lots of blues and golds in them. She had to admit that they were, without doubt, the most handsome wings she had seen so far.

"I haven't liked you all that much up to now," said Buster, at last.

"I know," said Emily. "Maybe it's a girl-boy thing."

"No," said Buster. "It's because I was jealous of you."

"Jealous of me?" said Emily, taken aback. "Why?"

"For inheriting this shop, for Fidget being so fond of you. Because you're a good detective."

Emily wasn't sure if she should say anything or not. There was one of those awkward silences that make you think that the room is full of jagged points.

"Do you like me?" Buster asked finally.

"I didn't at first," said Emily. "But I sort of do now. I think we make a good team."

Buster went to the curious cabinet and freed the key from the lock. He set it down on the floor, and it scurried away.

Buster watched it go.

"I must have done something right," he said, "to have been given my wings back."

"Yes," said Emily. "Go on, show me—fly."

And Buster did, a bit wobbly at first, but soon he got the hang of the thing, whizzing around the shop.

"Wooooo-hooo!" he shouted.

"Wow, that is something," said Emily as Buster turned somersaults in the air.

He landed next to her on the counter.

"Perhaps," he said, "being grown up isn't all it's cracked up to be."

"I think you are most probably right," said Emily. She paused. "I've worked out something."

"What?" asked Buster.

"Birdcage," said Emily. "It was Toff the Terrible who locked you in the birdcage."

Buster burst out laughing.

"How did you figure that?"

Emily smiled. "I can't go giving away all the tricks of the trade. And as for the spell that Toff was trying to use, you spotted it in that huge book in the library."

"Yes, but I needed you to point out that the lamp was useless without a genie," said Buster. "You are irritatingly good at being a detective."

"Come on, you two kippers, tea's ready," shouted Fidget.

In the living room, the magic lamp was sitting propped up on cushions, a blanket over its knees, holding a cup of steaming hot chocolate. It was telling the keys all about the awful time it'd had of it.

"I had such a fight to keep my lid on," it said. "I promise you, I would rather be melted down for gold than have a genie stuck inside me. They give you such terrible indigestion."

"There you are," said Lettice, as Buster walked in.

"You deserve to have your wings back, deary. Though still eleven, hmm. Never mind."

"I think I'm stranded at eleven," said Buster.

"Maybe one day you'll catch up," said Lettice. "But for now—"

"What are your plans, Lettice?" asked Emily quickly.

"After Pan's wedding, my tea trolley and I are out of here, deary. I'm not hanging around a day longer. I have places to see, fairies to visit, and"—she looked at Elvis—"an elf to return home to his mum and dad before he gets into another pickle."

"What about the magic lamp?" said Buster.

"What about it, deary?" asked Lettice.

"You can't leave me like this in my fragile state," said the lamp. "I mean any goblin, witch, or wizard might decide to stuff another genie in me and then what would happen?" It raised a hand to its lid. "I must be my own lamp with a lid that never opens."

Lettice hummed and hawed for a moment.

"I suppose you have a point, deary."

"It has, after all, been a very brave and noble lamp," said Emily.

"Noble! Oh, sweet mistress, how kind of you to say so," said the lamp.

Lettice took off her thick knit cardigan and found her wand once more.

This time she transformed her quiet gray dress into a silver gown. A diamond tiara sparkled on her head.

"That's amazing," said Emily.

"Yes it is, isn't it, deary?" said Lettice. "Now, lamp, are you ready?"

The magic lamp stood up, looking very solemn. Then it nodded. A whiz of light came from Lettice's wand, and the lamp seemed to judder and shake. It was done.

The lamp shone like new.

"At long last I am my own master!" And so saying, it kicked its legs up in the air. "Oh, sweet mistress, what joy—my Happily-Ever-After has arrived!"

Chapter Twenty-six

There is nothing like a wedding for a happy ending. Pan Smith wore her rainbow-colored wedding dress the day she married her sweetheart, Derek Lowe. Pan's mother, Pauline Smith, felt years younger since her hair had turned pink and her figure all apple-y. Her husband, Harry, couldn't have been more delighted.

As for Mr. Rollo, he was over the moon. The strangest thing had happened to him the day after he arrived home. He had received a lottery ticket in the post. Not just any old lottery ticket—it was the winning ticket for the Golden Jackpot. In short, Mr. Rollo was back in business.

Sergeant Litton hadn't been quite so lucky. He had

discovered that the five bags in fact contained not gold but horse poo, so the case was quietly closed and the horse poo was used on the town hall flower beds.

As far as the sergeant was concerned, the murder of Sir Walter Cross would remain an unsolved mystery.

Only Emily, Buster, and Fidget knew what had really happened in the case of the Three Pickled Herrings.

Fin

GOFISH

SALLY GARDNER

What did you want to be when you grew up?
I just wanted to grow up.

When did you realize you wanted to be a writer?
I was a storyteller at five years old. I never thought I could be a writer because I can't spell.

What's your most embarrassing childhood memory?
I was seven, and my knickers fell down round my ankles in Holborn. I stepped out of them and left them on the pavement.

Did you play sports as a kid?
At school I had to play lacrosse. The main point of the game seemed to be to break other girls' noses. So I ran the wrong way down the pitch and scored in our own goal. After that, I didn't have to play again.

What book is on your nightstand now?

Two YA books: *We Were Liars* by E. Lockhart and *Rooftoppers* by Katherine Rundell. I'm enjoying them both enormously. And *The Rosie Project* by Graeme Simsion makes me laugh out loud. I'm also reading *A Great and Monstrous Thing* by Jerry White as I'm currently researching eighteenth-century London for a new book.

Where do you write your books?

I write on a 1940s desk that I was told was once in the offices of the Ministry of War. It's heavy and solid and was designed so that whoever was working at it could shelter underneath it during an air raid rather than run down to the air raid shelter. I love the drumming noise it makes when I'm typing—to me it's the sound of a chapter going well.

What is your favorite part of *Operation Bunny*?

When Emily escapes from the Dashwoods, and she and Fidget catch the train to London. It is the beginning of her new, magical life.

What are some of your favorite fairy tales?

Beauty and the Beast, *Rapunzel*, and *The Tinderbox*, which inspired my YA book *Tinder*.

Which of your characters is most like you?

There's quite a lot of me in Fidget.

What makes you laugh out loud?
The many mishaps that befall me.

What is your favorite word?
Discombobulate.

What's your favorite song?
"Woodman, Spare That Tree" by Phil Harris.

What was your favorite book when you were a kid? Do you have a favorite book now?
Great Expectations by Charles Dickens.

What's your favorite TV show or movie?
I enjoyed *Game of Thrones*. And loved Wes Anderson's film *The Grand Budapest Hotel*.

If you could travel in time, where would you go and what would you do?
London in the eighteenth century and the first half of the nineteenth century. I would see absolutely everything—all the wonderful buildings that have since disappeared. I would want to meet painter and social critic William Hogarth and, most of all, Charles Dickens.

What's the best advice you have ever received about writing?
Judith Elliot was my first editor at Orion. She told me that everyone can sing, but few have a voice. She convinced me that I had a voice and could write.

If you were a superhero, what would your superpower be?
I live on the fifth floor of a block of flats with no lift. It would be handy if I could fly.

What do you consider to be your greatest accomplishment?
Winning the Carnegie Medal for my book *Maggot Moon*.

What do you wish you could do better?
Be more organized.

GO FISH

DAVID ROBERTS

What did you want to be when you grew up?
I wanted to be a policeman because my dad was a policeman.

When did you realize you wanted to be an illustrator?
When I realized that someone would actually pay me to draw.

What's your most embarrassing childhood memory?
On the way to a Christmas party at the local church when I was six, I slipped in dog poo and sat down right on top of it! I had to go to my gran's house, who washed my trousers (poor Gran!) whilst I sat reading a book in my bright orange underpants. I missed the party. I've never liked dogs since.

What's your favorite childhood memory?
Holidays in our caravan in North Wales.

What was your first job, and what was your "worst" job?

First job was washing hair in the local salon in my home village. I was fourteen.

Worst job was frying eggs in a kitchen in a factory. After the thirty-seventh egg, I thought, *There must be more to life than this!* I never went back.

How did you celebrate publishing your first book?

My first book was *Frankie Stein's Robot* by Roy Apps. I couldn't believe I'd actually been given the chance to do a children's book, and I was made up when I saw it on the shelves of the bookshops. I celebrated with my brother Paul, whom I dedicated the book to, and my friend Paul and my flatmate Julia. I'm sure champagne was involved, although I can't remember.

Where do you work on your illustrations?

I have a room in my apartment with all my books in it, a flat file cabinet to store my work, and lots of pictures on the wall to inspire me.

Where do you find inspiration for your illustrations?

I find inspiration from my favorite artists and illustrators, music, watching people, surface patterns on cloth and wallpaper, and amazing landscapes like the Faroe Islands.

What was it like to work on *Operation Bunny*?
I was in New York at the time, living on the twenty-second floor of an apartment building. I would sit in the window and listen to all the noise from the street below. It was a nice escape to go into the strange world of fairies, witches, bunnies, and magic lamps.

Is it easier to illustrate bunnies or herrings?
I don't mind either, though I suppose I can get a bit more expression into a bunny than a herring—especially a pickled one!

Where do you go for peace and quiet?
I don't really like quiet and so have a radio in every room.

What makes you laugh out loud?
My friend Matt makes me laugh out loud the most when he pretends to be Liza Minnelli!

What's your favorite song?
"They Don't Know" by Tracey Ullman. I bought this single on my first trip to London in 1983.

Who is your favorite fictional character?
I recently illustrated *The Wind in the Willows*, which was an enormous pleasure, and I fell in love with the characters of Ratty and Mole. I've always loved the idea of owning a rowing boat and being able to row every day on a river, so I'd kind of rather like to be Ratty.

If you could travel in time, where would you go and what would you do?
I'd go back to 1979 and buy myself a ticket for Kate Bush's first concert at the Liverpool Empire Theatre.

What's the best advice you have ever received about illustrating?
Don't be afraid of the white expanse of paper.

What would you do if you ever stopped illustrating?
I really can't do anything else, but if I didn't have to earn a living, I'd spend a lot of time knitting. And I'd love to keep bees.

What do you consider to be your greatest accomplishment?
Every time somebody sends me a new text and asks me to illustrate his or her book.

What do you wish you could do better?
Illustration!

What would your readers be most surprised to learn about you?
I quite like knitting!

What's the strangest dream you've ever had?
When I was a child, I used to have a dream that there were furry fluorescent pink and orange snakes in my bed.

What was your favorite thing about school?
I never, ever liked school.

What was your least favorite thing about school?
Having to go!

If you could travel anywhere in the world, where would you go and what would you do?
I'm planning a trip to Svalbard, a Norwegian island in the Arctic Circle. I hope I get to see the Northern Lights.

Who is your favorite artist?
David Hockney.

What is your favorite medium to work in?
I work in pen, ink, watercolor, and pencil.

What was your favorite book or comic/graphic novel when you were a kid? What's your current favorite?
My favorite book was and is *A Hole Is to Dig* by Ruth Krauss and Maurice Sendak. I love the simplicity of the little line drawings that have so much expression and feeling.

What challenges do you face in the artistic process, and how do you overcome them?
I'm always working to a brief, which is the text, and the biggest challenge is deciding what is the best

thing to illustrate. What is going to help tell the story but also work around the story? Sometimes you have to look behind the scenes and read between the lines.

Things are about to get
INTERESTING for the Wings & Co.
Fairy Detective Agency.

How will Emily and her friends deal with
a missing giant, a seaside murder, a stolen diamond,
and a TV talent show?

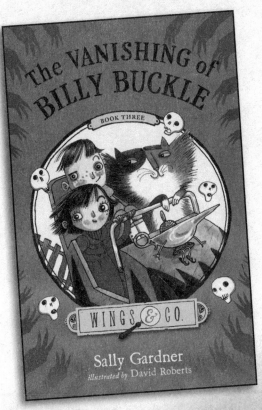

The VANISHING of
BILLY BUCKLE

BOOK THREE

WINGS & CO.

Sally Gardner
illustrated by David Roberts

*Keep reading for a sneak peek
of the next adventure.*

It had started one wet Monday when Fidget told Emily
that his old mate, the giant Billy Buckle, needed someone to look after his daughter, Primrose, for a weekend.

"Why?" said Emily.

So many strange things had happened since Emily
first met Fidget that the idea he knew a giant didn't
strike her as all that odd.

"Because he plays the bassoon in the Sad Dads'
Band, and they are having a reunion gig."

"Why can't he take his daughter with him?" Emily
had asked.

"Because of the Bog-Eyed Loader," replied Fidget.

"The Bog-Eyed Loader," repeated Emily.

"Yep. He lives in a cave in the Valley of Doom,"
said Fidget. Fidget was seated in his favorite armchair,
knitting himself a fish-shaped hat, while outside the

rain poured. It had not been, Emily thought, much of a summer.

"I've never heard of it. Is it near Podgy Bottom?" she asked.

"Frazzle a fishmonger! It's nowhere near here. It's in the land of the giants," said Fidget.

"How do you know Billy Buckle?" asked Emily.

"Billy was a great friend of Miss String," said Fidget.

Anything to do with the late Miss Ottoline String always had Emily's full attention.

Fidget and Miss String had first met Billy Buckle many moons ago, when the fairy detectives were investigating the Case of the Missing Harp. After that, the giant had often visited them for tea, until he'd moved away.

"He came for tea?" said Emily, impressed. She tried to imagine a giant sitting in one of Miss String's deck chairs and drinking out of an impossibly small teacup. "Where did he move to?"

"We never knew, my little ducks," said Fidget. "That's the thing with giants. They have very long legs. Anyway, now, out of the blue, I've heard from him."

"How?"

"There is a postal service," said Fidget.

"You mean letters? With stamps? Not e-mail?"

"Well, not stamps exactly. Not e-mail exactly. Some-times, my little ducks," said Fidget kindly, "I have to pinch myself to remember you are not a fairy."

"Oh dear," said Emily. "I wish I was. It might make things easier. For a start, Buster wouldn't be so horrible to me."

"Never mind," said Fidget. "I wouldn't change a squid about you."

"What exactly is a Bog-Eyed Loader?" asked Emily.

"He is an ogre, most of the time, and fierce to boot, with a nasty habit of shape-shifting."

"Oh," said Emily. "Like, turning into a . . . a . . . hippopotamus?"

"Yep. That sort of thing."

"Or . . . a fish?"

"If he did that," said Fidget, "I would sardine-tin him lickety-split."

A twitchy look came over Fidget's whiskers, which usually meant he felt he had answered enough questions.

But Emily was determined to find out more before Fidget went off in search of fish-paste sandwiches.

"So that's why Billy Buckle isn't taking his daughter."

"Spot on the fishcake," said Fidget. "The Bog-Eyed Loader has been known to take travelers prisoner. Once he caught a wizard's wife and wouldn't let her go until the wizard agreed to teach the Bog-Eyed Loader some spells. A magic spell in the hands of the Bog-Eyed Loader is a very dangerous thing indeed. There is no knowing what he might do with it."

Emily had wanted to ask why Primrose couldn't stay with her mother if the Valley of Doom was so un-safe, and about what else the Bog-Eyed Loader could do, but she saw that Fidget was lost in fishy dreams. He wandered off, muttering to himself about fish-paste sandwiches.

She tried to learn more about the ogre from Buster. He was sprawled on his bed, looking at a magazine. He glanced up at Emily.

"Do you think my clothes look old-fashioned?" he said. "Has the time come for a revamp?"

"What do you know about the Bog-Eyed Loader?" Emily asked.

"Don't go saying his name 'round here. It isn't lucky," said Buster.

"Why not?" asked Emily.

"Because he can foggle a fairy."

"Foggle?"

"Oh," said Buster. "Yet another of the many things you don't know about fairies." He looked up. "You do know that bats make a high-pitched noise that echoes back at them, so they can find their way in the dark?"

"Yes," said Emily. "I do, actually." She was rather interested in bats.

"Well, fairies have the same sort of thing. And the Bog-Eyed Loader can foggle it up, which isn't good."

"You mean, the fairies bang into things and can't find their way around?"

But by now Buster was bored with the subject.

"Look at these sneakers," he said. "They're wicked. There are gold ones and silver ones—even sneakers with flashing lights. I think I would look supercool in those."

Emily sighed. Why wouldn't anyone tell her more about the Bog-Eyed Loader? He sounded interesting, and since they had solved the Case of the Three Pickled Herrings, not much interesting had happened. Life had settled into a sleepy pace. The weather had become warmer, the trees had turned green, and Buster went out flying . . . a lot.

The magic lamp, which had once belonged to the witch Harpella but had since turned over a new leaf, now spent hours in front of the mirror, shining itself and encouraging the keys to keep a better hygiene routine. Emily sometimes wondered if the title Keeper of the Keys shouldn't belong to the magic lamp rather than her, for the keys never did a thing she asked them to do—like opening drawers in the curious cabinets and returning wings to their rightful owners. They seemed to listen only to the lamp, and they followed it around wherever it went. As for Doughnut, the miniature dachshund who had adopted the detectives during the Case of the Three Pickled Herrings, he slept most of the day or waited to be taken for a walk. Fidget sat knitting more and more fish scarves, hats, mittens, and sweaters.

He had even knitted a dress for Emily in the shape of a fish. Emily was very proud of it and wore it quite often.

So the most exciting event in ages was the arrival of Billy Buckle and Primrose. They had turned up one muggy July evening two weeks earlier. Emily's first glimpse of Billy had been a pair of very large red shoes at the shop's entrance. Above them were striped socks and tartan trousers. Billy's height reached the second floor, and as for Primrose, she was only just able to squeeze through the shop door.

Billy Buckle had crouched down to talk to Fidget.

"It's very decent of you, dude," he said. "The boys are right chuffed I am going to be there. At last, the Sad Dads' Band will be back together again."

"How long will you be gone?" Fidget asked.

"Oh, a couple of days at the most. If it wasn't for the Bog-Eyed Loader, I'd take my Primrose with me. But there you go—it just isn't safe. I can look after myself, but she's only a little thing."

He gave Primrose a kiss, told her to be good, and went on his way.

Since then, there had been no sign of Billy Buckle.

Fidget made the usual inquiries, and letters had been exchanged with the other Sad Dads. All anyone knew was that Billy Buckle had played two sets with the band before leaving to pick up Primrose. Fidget had even placed an ad in *Fairy World International*. It said simply that anyone with information as to the whereabouts of Billy Buckle should contact Wings & Co.

Emily asked Fidget quietly if the Bog-Eyed Loader could be responsible. More letters flew here and there.

"Definitely not," said Fidget. "Billy disappeared before he made it to the Valley of Doom."

Still, no one had replied to the ad.

This, Emily decided, was a case for Wings & Co. And they needed to solve it quickly, for Primrose was growing daily.